THE ALIEN WORLD
THE COMPLETE ILLUSTRATED GUIDE

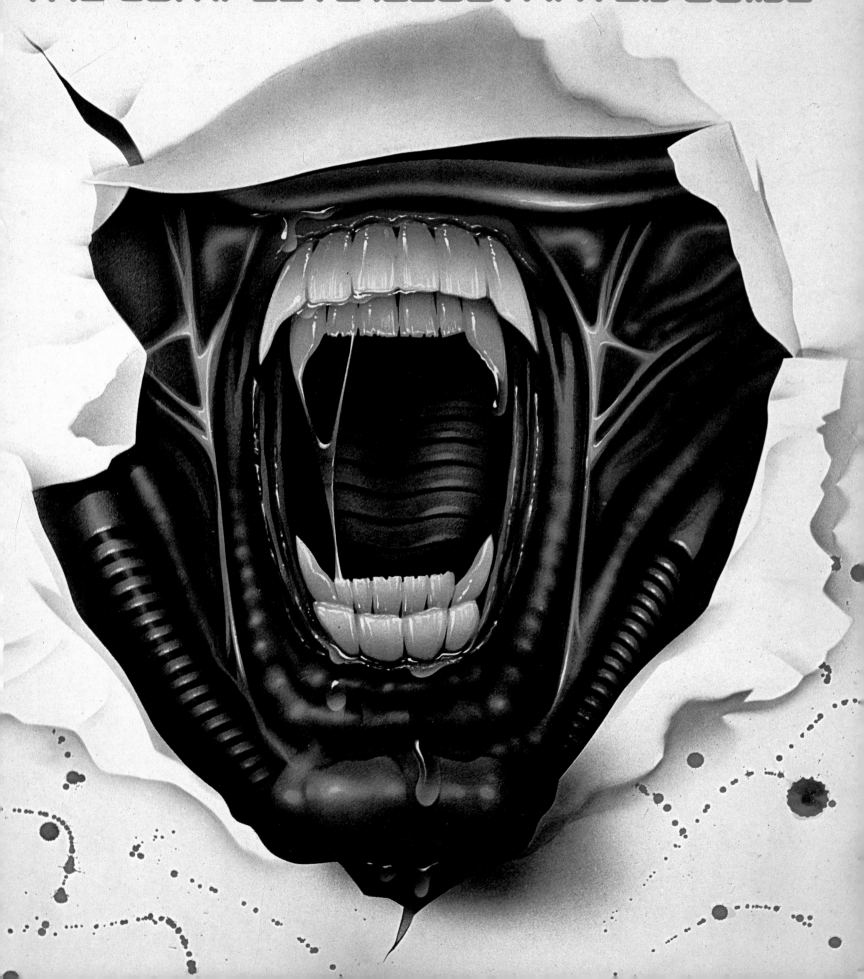

THE ALIEN
THE COMPLETE ILLUSTRATED GUIDE

STEVEN EISLER

CRESCENT BOOKS
New York

© MCMLXXX Octopus Books Limited
First English Edition Published 1980
by Octopus Books Limited,
59 Grosvenor Street, London W1

This edition is published by Crescent Books,
a division of Crown Publishers, Inc.

Produced by Mandarin Publishers Limited,
22A Westlands Road,
Quarry Bay, Hong Kong

Printed in Hong Kong

Eisler, Steven

The Alien World:
the complete illustrated guide
L Title
PZ4.L3457 AI 1980 (PS3555.I87)
813'.5'4 79-23746
ISBN 0 517 30560 7

CONTENTS

INTRODUCTION

With every passing century, as Humankind pushes the frontier of space exploration almost to the ends of the Universe, the available information on life on other worlds increases at a staggering rate. Although the great expansion outward to the stars occurred in the fourth millennium After Eagle (AE), at which time more than 60 intelligent life forms were discovered, in the 5000 years since, as the sphere of Human contact has extended to a radius of 77 million lEons (light eons), many hundreds more intelligent alien creatures have been reported, documented, and even brought home as emissaries. Unquestionably, the Five Sectors are only five of hundreds; the Known Universe is but a fraction of one percent of the total Universe. It will be many millions of years, unless a major breakthrough in warp drive technology occurs, before a solitary stardriver orbits the last star in the Universe, and peers outwards into God's eternal darkness, looking, literally, beyond the end of space and time and matter.

All of which, when considered, might make it slightly presumptuous of me to call my book *A Complete Guide to the Alien World.* Even as I write, the odds of yet another race possessed of creativity and self awareness being discovered are one in a hundred. By the time my words are processed by CompuGraph LitService Central (after the statutory Earth year in traditional book form) and telefaxed onto billions of Home-Print Consoles, more than 50 expeditions will have returned to the Human Sector. Many centuries displaced from their own times, sturdy explorers from our historical past, confused and terrified by our world, new language and new ideologies, will nevertheless bear with them the details of hundreds of life forms, as yet only guessed at. There can never be a truly complete guide to the Universe of non-Human aliens.

For this reason, perhaps, available records of life in the Universe are startlingly few. Recently, as I researched the Narathnian Sector, preparatory to compiling a program of their ancient legends and stories, it came home to me just how out of date, how sparse, and how specialized were the accounts of the span of the alien presence in God's Back Yard, as the early explorers called the Universe. Every alien race that is reported by the stardrivers is usually recorded on tempufax, ultimately to be filed in Life Sources Central on Andaluce (Antarres III). Interest in obscure, usually technologically primitive alien races, is very limited. Details on the main life forms certainly occur in abundance, but usually are not updated. More often than not they are printed by Ursan Education Publishers Ltd, an agreeably vast, conscientious, bulk specialized publishing firm, with a print availability capable of supplying to the University worlds and, of course, Earth itself, with its elite population of the idle curious. And the great, if over-rated, *Out-Thrust Encyclopedia of World Knowledge,* of which the *Encyclopedia Galactica* is a sub-section, was last revised in 9867 AE, nearly 40 generations ago, and certainly before the discovery of the Qa'Qal'Orq Gestalt. Since it is a book of over 20 billion word units, originally compiled by one man working alone, living in the Terran city state of NorLond, it is unsurprising that the great work has been allowed to decay into obscurity. It will need the resources of an energetic and rich association to raise funds and recruit millions of researchers before the work can be revised from beginning to end.

There is, therefore, no single accessible work that attempts to contain a complete guide to the social and racial structure of the Universe, a beginning point, a reference source that, although inadequately detailed in itself, may indicate at a glance the span of life, the spread of life, and the areas of most rapid evolution of life. This is the aim of my guide. Every alien race of technological importance is recorded; every evolution zone is recorded; every race that you, the receiver, are likely to experience in your life time, in one form or another, is mentioned. Naturally enough there is no room, and possibly no need, to document every race of 'emerging self awareness', from, say, the Human equivalent of the early Stone Age until the first Stellar Age, (2987 AD by the old reckoning of time). Those were primitive eras. Humankind was still struggling to fully understand its embryonic intelligence, and was entering the final cycle of Wars. These had begun with the Iron Age Wars of territorial acquisition, passed through the Machine Wars of the middle ages and the Paranoia Wars of the 20th century, and terminated in the Wars of Self Righteousness in the early 21st century. These times are of limited importance in any race's history, and except in rare instances, have not been included in this account. As a baseline for evolutionary intelligence, I have used Bertoleggi's Machine Fabrication Equivalent, concentrating on life forms with an MFE of 10 or more, that is, those races who have advanced to the discovery of warp or star drive, and know what to do with it.

Throughout the *Guide* references to time have been equated with the time scale of the Human Sector. Thus, for example, the foundation of the Qa'Qal'Orq Hegemony, in their own time of 73 of the Life of the OverLord Grath, is dated 2788 BE, the third millennium before the landing of the *Eagle* the first primitive, fire-powered void car – (space ship is hardly appropriate) – upon Earth's satellite, Van Halsen's Land (or Lunar as it was once called). It had occurred to me to date events in the Universe from the Final Jovian War, and the first Human attempt to breach the time wall of the Universe. And it was suggested, by students of history, that I should refer all dates to 2000 years before the landing of the *Eagle,* to the visitation to Earth of the Qa'Qal'Orq Gestalt in the form of the Human God of Turin. It was even suggested that I should make the second tentative exploration of Earth by that Gestalt mind, in the prophesied Three Brothers – the Kennedys – the starting date. I have resisted the temptation. In cases where the time period of life of an alien species was immense I have cited merely the appropriate number of Earth years. When events occurred close

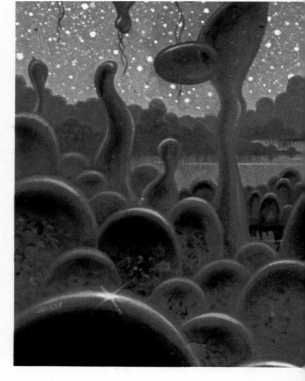

Life in many forms: the five sectors of the universe known to man are but five of hundreds, and the vast variety of life he has encountered is just a fraction of the life that must exist. We are most comfortable with the humanoid species, such as the Narathanan Astero Trader (top), but humanoids comprise only eleven per cent of the known galactic species. Machine life, such as the Igrafralexi (bottom right) abounds in all universal sectors, and poses particular problems to the illogical-thinking human race. The most intriguing life form that man yet has to contact fully is the Gestalt Mind of the Qa'-Qual'-Org. These alien forms seem to have a full appreciation of human Gestalt psychological theory as developed on the planet earth during the mid period of the twentieth century, but they present a considerable problem to humans.

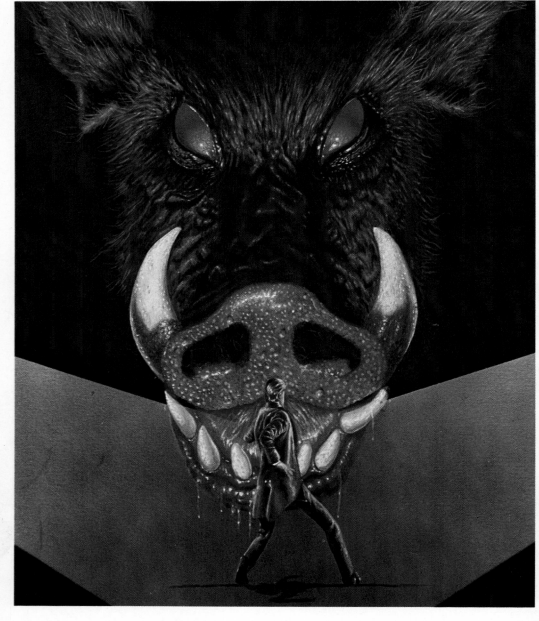

Close relationships between Man and Alien take many forms; several colonial worlds, unusual for their adoption of historical modes of dress, enjoy harmonious relations with the local intelligent life, such as the hog-like Carnakpril of Ghost V, and the winged Bladwij of Cyrana B, to name but a few of the Aliens we have classified.

to a known and recorded moment of Earth history, I have made that comparison. Otherwise the time scale for the Universe is referred to on the basis of today being the year 10673 AE.

It is my hope that the *Guide* will be updated every few years to include in its pages the new understanding and new records of the more significant alien species which will doubtless be discovered as Humans travel further into the Great Back Yard. As an introduction I feel the work will be invaluable. It will help creche supervisors on hundreds of worlds to educate the young of our species, before they are returned to the doting, irresponsible 'control' of their parents; and it will form a solid factual groundwork for students of the alien, who will have an opportunity to experience the structure of the whole Five Sectors before losing direction, and depth, in any of the immensely specialized tomes that deal so exclusively with so little.

I make no apology if I resort to 'storytelling', for it is among the legends and heroic tales of many of the far travelled

and aged races of the Sectors that we find the greatest clues, and most poignant information, about how it was out there among the stars, when the Human race was still mining flint and living in fear of the winds and rains. Since each Sector is dominated by one race, I have concentrated upon that race and attempted to trace its links and associations with the other intelligent species in its Sector.

Finally, a back yard that covers so many millions of lEons is a large yard to play in. It could well be that I have overlooked some important member of the alien world, and should include it at the earliest possible juncture. It is also of interest to me to learn of any legend or ancient tale or mythology concerning the alien life forms I have gazetted. Wherever you live, on Earth or on the far-flung, climatically engineered worlds of Starhaven VII, whether you eke out an existence in asbestos cities on the Fire Fall worlds of Bootes, or swim with genetically engineered gills in the salt seas of Alpha Aquitania, if you know something that I don't, please do not hesitate to fax it through to me.

DOMINANT INTELLIGENCE: OISIR-RAXXLA
REPTILIAFORM INTELLIGENCE, GIGANTIC
FORMS; 2,300 PSI-PROJECTORS X INTELLIGENT LIFE
NO. OF GALAXIES 189TH YEARS OF DOMINANCE 780,000

Boris Vallejo

Left: A male Oisir-Raxxla surgically engineered for close physical combat. Note the nose horn and the sabre claws grafted on the dexterous and manipulable fingers. The Human Federation maintains a friendly but distant relationship with the Oisir-Raxxla whom they have nicknamed the 'tyraks'. These creatures have a very high intelligence and their violent tendencies derive mainly from a need to establish the structure known as the Talmor Lens on as many worlds as possible. Above: An immature young Oisir-Raxxla enjoying the sort of symbiotic relationship that adult tyraks encourage. The girl is a Human from a colony world, probably in the Null Zone between Oisir-Raxxla and Human dominated space. The teenage tyrak provides a fast mount, an efficient hunting machine and, of course, comradeship. The human is almost certainly plucking at bone-drilling parasites from the exoskeletal layer of the tyrak's flesh.

That part of the Known Universe that lies on the Human side of the Night Wall, the immense barrier of time and space distortion that has resulted from the passage of a subspace galaxy, is called the Oisir-Raxxla Sector, after the dominant race. This biozone comprises less than 2000 galaxies, clustered tightly almost into a circle, bordered by the Tharana Void and the Delvonne Void, where there is instability in the fabric of space itself. It is separated from the Human Sector by the Urgenirk Darks, a straggling line of vast black holes, lined up along 40 million lEons, drawing dense strands of dark gas from the Night Wall. This has meant that Human contact with the Oisir-Raxxla has been minimal, despite the proximity of the Sectors, and no Human colonies have been established within the region. However, the Oisir-Raxxla have themselves populated some three million worlds of the Sector and 2300 other intelligent life forms are known to coexist with them. Of these 12 have an MFE (Machine Fabri-

cation Equivalent) of 11 or more.

The Oisir-Raxxla are classified as gigantiform, exosketeletal reptilioid analogues. They are warlike beings with an immensely advanced technology and an overwhelming desire for conquest. This has driven them into 17 major space wars, including participation in the Interspace Wars of '93, the contest for the mineral resources of the Kalpecca Star Shallows fought between the Human Federation and the Null Zone Empire of the Yulix. The reasons for Oisir-Raxxla mania for conquest and violence are unusual, and will be discussed later.

The life form itself arose in a globular cluster, the so-called Samarandara Pearls, first described by Ahmed Samarandara as he successfully navigated his probeship through the Urgenirk Darks to discover the new zone beyond. Their planet of origin was a small, barren world (called Zaath, which means home in their language) which taxed their evolving intelligence to the utmost.

Within 600 generations of their emergence from primitivism, the Oisir-Raxxla had discovered the basic principles of time space phase linked travel (thruspace), and had subdued and colonized the 130 habitable worlds in the cluster. Only 40 generations later, they had conquered the galaxy of which their satellite was a part, and were spreading out in all directions into their Sector. By Human standards the entire conquest of the home galaxy had taken nearly four million years. The generation time of the Oisir-Raxxla is 6000 years, although in the last four million years a shortening to 3000 years has been recorded. This tremendous life span was evolved in order to capitalize upon a constantly barren world. Only periodically during its 1000-year orbit about its primary did Zaath flourish and release crystal-locked water into the atmosphere and dried river beds. It was only in these occasionally fertile conditions that the dormant life forms could emerge from their underground cysts. The Oisir-Raxxla alone managed to evolve a monitoring device on their tails, an eye-like, hydrosensitive organ that enabled them to awake earliest from hibernation. They became the dominant species, and a form of self awareness was inevitable.

The Caesar syndrome: an urge to conquer

The whole reason for the Oisir-Raxxla obsession with conquest was not, as has sometimes been suggested, to exploit mineral wealth, nor to indoctrinate other life forms with their beliefs, but rather to recruit slave labour. A conquest could be short lived, as with the insect-like Yulissia, inhabitants of the world Yulanda, an oceanless planet whose crust was one immense honeycomb of warrens and underground breeding places. The Oisir-Raxxla conquered the Yulissian army in less than 20 years – an instant by their own reckoning. The conquest happened so fast that information about the deployment of Yulissian war machines had not even been processed by the Raxxlan Command computer by the time the world was subdued.

On the other hand, a conquest might take many hundreds of years, as with the attack and eventual enslavement of the Ithnaxi that inhabit the five snowy worlds of the Ithnaxas system. Giant, bear-like creatures, the Ithnaxi had all descended from tiny arboreal creatures that originally inhabited the smallest of the five worlds. No bigger than a Human hand, the Ithnaxi originals had developed a stone-based technology, harnessing the energy locked in crystals of dinathium, a common element in Ithnaxian granite. Their spaceships were hollowed-out boulders that had fallen from cliffs and volcanoes. In these bizarre space dugouts they moved from world to world and moon to moon of their closely clustered system. However, their machine technology was very limited, a crucial factor in understanding the difficulty the Oisir-Raxxla experienced in conquering them.

The Oisir-Raxxla have the capability of transmitting their minds into robots. They can also influence and even become mac-

Above: *A particularly nasty piece of Raxxlan robotics. This skeletal machine was designed to spread alarm and despondancy among races that the Oisir-Raxxla wanted to subdue without going to all the bother of genocide. This robot, which would normally be a MOLE class model well up on the ISAC (Integrated Sabotage/Assassination Capacity) scale, was sent to selected races disguised as a representative of the most holy caste. When a sufficiently large group of worshippers had gathered, the robot would run beserk or occasionally explode.*
Right: *A bull Ithnaxi is a vicious creature, able to disembowel a Human at a stroke.*

hines. This ability was artificially developed during the Quintharx Hegemony, (45200 BE), when a scientific elite ruled Zaath, and the military leaders were obsessed with avoiding the necessity of direct contact between the Oisir-Raxxla and any other alien form. Techniques of mind projection had been tried in the past, and were now developed to such an extent that the disembodied awareness could attach itself to controls, circuits and crystals in practically any machine construct. Thus, during their slow conquest of the Sector they could invade a world by taking over the luxury and essential machinery of the world, and turning it against its creators. Societies whose computers and mechanical aids are on the side of the enemy cannot survive for long. And it was not just the more obvious machines that were controlled: public transport machines, automatic sewage disposal, power consoles, hearing aids, everything could be possessed by the mindforce of the

Oisir-Raxxla.

The watery world of Chorep, with its advanced amphibia forms, was conquered by the Oisir-Raxxla mindforce taking over their televisual machines and bombarding the gentle, entertainment-obsessed creatures with a Human century (a Chorep year) of terrifying propaganda. The pastoral world of Peridi Almar had long before been turned into a single, huge field of the corn-like crop *erzac* by the humanoid Almarians. These natural farmers had developed a machine technology, but had remained mentally backward, content to ride their colossal harvesters (three kilometres long) about the planet, meeting only occasionally at the volcanic lakes where they found water, and the rudimentary cities and mining towns of their world. The meetings were for the purposes of mating. Resultant young completed a circuit of the world in the parental harvester, before being sent off to wander through the *erzac*, moving

Michael Whelan

Graham Wildridge

through the gigantic corn until tall enough (over 200 metres) to see above the stalks. Then came the contesting with the older harvesters for their machines, the winning and the killing, and the continuance of the harvesting life, riding the harvesters, and gathering the crop for disposal at the volcanic spaceports. When the Oisir-Raxxla assessed the invasion needs, they realized that conquest here would be as easy as turning the harvesters into sentient and uncooperative beings. They devastated the Almarians.

It must be said that much of the Raxxlan plan of conquest was bloodless in conception. Once the purpose of the invasion was over, the aliens would leave, and the planet was allowed to return to its original way of life. This was never actually the case. Since, more often than not, the Oisir-Raxxla were never seen, myths and legends grew up in abundance, mainly in the religious sections of society, in an attempt to explain what had happened. The ancient invaders were perceived as 'devils' and other supernatural visitations. Prophets and other holy creatures would often appear to combat them and the path of religious evolution was often diverted.

The Talmor Lens: a time net

What was it that drove the Oisir-Raxxla to systematically enslave whole galaxies, however bloodlessly? They wanted to build Talmor Lenses. They wanted to enslave time itself. At a time when the Human race had not yet evolved beyond the tiny, lemur-like ancestor that lived on the African plains, the Oisir-Raxxla were still a peace-loving, rather naive race, who had journeyed beyond their own galaxy by just a few hundred light years, and had established primarily friendly contact with those alien races that they had encountered. Planetfall on the world we know as Jodethum changed the destiny of the Oisir-Raxxla totally.

Even then Jodethum was a dead world, a ruined place, covered with the scars of war and the remnants of cities that had once spanned its continents. For thousands of years the Oisir-Raxxla explored the vast caverns, the sky-high structures, the orbiting satellite cities, their interiors preserved in a state of dust-free mummification. They learned much of the creatures that had lived here and had ruled the Universe so many millions of years before. They learned secrets that led to the development of what we would call the warp drive, the space mechanism which allows the almost instantaneous traversing of vast distances of space. They discovered an ancient wisdom that had never been applied by the elf-like inhabitants of Jodethum. It was the secret not just of stabilizing time, but of moving through time, of controlling time in a way beyond even the power of the great Gestalt on Hiraldion. Humankind had felt that they were close to discovering the principle, for occasionally the warp drive would fail and ships would pass into the distant past or future, but we could not control the effect finely enough for it to be of use. To protect this mind-boggling secret, one of the greatest races

18

Left: Building the Talmor Lens. A Raxxla taskship orbits a deserted world, building satellite connections with the machine on the planetary surface below. This planet is a small, sterile asteroid-type. These were favoured locations, since there was no need for conquest. *Above:* A ruined harvester abandoned on Peridi Almar, a world conquered by the Oisir-Raxxla. *Far left:* A part of the Talmor Lens, build on the world Capralax VII. This is an 'edge-stabiliser', designed to hold the underspace tensions of five pyramidal lenses in control.

that had ever walked the star fields had waged civil war and ultimately destroyed itself.

It took 40 generations for the Oisir-Raxxla to decipher the coded formulae and find what they must do to bring time under their control; and the answer was daunting. It involved the building of lenses and stabilizers not just across their own world, but on worlds that spanned the enormity of the Universe itself. A million lenses, a million stabilizers, a million power harnesses, a million structures to twist the flow of space, and focus everything on the Saramandara Pearls; and when it was done, time would cease to exist in that globular cluster, and the Oisir-Raxxla would have a haven from the ravages and destructive fingers of time. They would have a place from which they could explore and enjoy all of time, each and every wonder of each and every

Universe that had ever been or ever will be.

It was a dream that came to obsess them and to demand all but a fraction of the energy and economy of their race. They began their task of conquering and building, a task they continue to this day. For thousands of years, architectural and mathematical expeditions spread outwards into the farthest reaches of the Raxxlan Known Universe, gradually constructing the machine that would focus the Universal force into that far distant point. The expeditions never knew their home world, they knew only the Task; generations were born, lived and died on the huge Task Ships as they sought the correct locations for the various parts of the machine. And at a time in our distant past, one such ship found Earth, and realized it was the ideal place to build a set of stabilizers.

There was no machine technology in

Graham Wildridge

that time on our planet, and the Oisir-Raxxla built machines in the image of the men below . . . taller, stronger, controlled from above, the robots walked among men, and began the legends of the gods; they were remembered, in time, as the god 'Horus'. The place the Oisir-Raxxla had chosen to start the work was the country known today as Egypt, and here they found a society ready-made for their work, with an elite royalty overseeing a rigidly stratified population. It was the work of no more than four dynasties to convince the pharoahs to build their tombs as pyramids, conforming to the various dimensions required for the Talmor Lens. Without the presence of a technology that could produce non-corrosible metals, stone was used, and the stabilizers stood for thousands of years. Only one small fact marred the achievement of the Oisir-Raxxla on Earth. No one aboard the Task Ship had been alive when the journey had begun. Mindlessly they had obeyed the sacred directives, slowly forgetting the purpose of the mission, and the grand design that would result as its end point. Slowly, too, the significance and importance of shape was twisted and confused and ultimately lost. They built the stabilizers, the pyramids of Earth, in the easy way, with the points *toward* the stars; a disastrous mistake for the Oisir-Raxxla, and the beginning of the end of their dream.

The Sirens of Ivixor B

Within ten light years of the Urgenirk Darks, where the black holes sweep through the Oisir-Raxxla Sector, lies the giant red sun Ivixor B. It is still hot enough to support a shell of 40 planetary bodies, and the life forms that live upon them. Ivixor B was first recorded by Chesowaya Samarandara, great grandson of the stardriver who had first penetrated the Urgenirk Darks and documented so many of the galactic systems beyond. The following underspaced message from the younger Samarandara was picked up at Obethurey Station:

> . . . a sun not dissimilar to Algol, but with the fires of hell burning from its surface . . . 43 worlds, clustered in a narrow plane, and most of them giants, their gaseous atmospheres curling wraith-like into the void . . . colours, so beautiful, the richness of reds and purples, and the scores of rocky moons . . . ruins, I think . . . yes, ruins, the hulls of ships and stations, the closer I go the more I see, thousands, millions of wrecks . . . the singing is louder now, a strangely haunting whistling through the transceiver sets; the rubidax crystals have changed colour and when I cool them they emit this strange song, all scales and strange combinations of

> notes . . . I feel oddly drawn towards the world, an image in my mind tells me my great grandfather is here . . . I can sense his ship, lying in the void, and his voice seems to be calling to me through the song voices of the worlds . . . I must go closer and seek him, but the wrecked ships are clustered so closely about each world that I am in danger of collision. End report.

This was also the end of the young Samarandara, but his report had been monitored and in later years, with the cooperation of the Oisir-Raxxla, the deadly sun of Ivixor B was investigated by a larger team of ships, equipped with elaborate automatic escape mechanisms. They discovered the Kiiry, a race of beings living in the upper atmospheres of seven of the 43 worlds, the seven largest planets.

The Kiiry are gigantic, medusoid creatures, which float through the hydrogen seas of the worlds on gas-filled bells, trailing limbs down into the denser atmosphere. Some energy tendrils are more than 2000 kilometres long. At certain times of their lives the Kiiry change form, becoming long and spindle shaped, grotesquely enormous beasts, swollen to a length of 100 kilometres or more. They drift upwards and, using energy stored in special locomotor cells in their teguments, swim through the void of space between worlds. It is likely that the Kiiry were never bound to the one world of their origin, but colonized the other six giant worlds in the same way that a herd of beasts might spread out to occupy the whole of a river valley. Their 'singing' on subspace frequencies, is a deliberate attempt to seduce passing ships into their field of influence. They can detect the subspace emissions from ships and repeat the 'tunes', creating an oddly hypnotic effect on most spacefaring races. Ships are attracted into the solar influence zone of Ivixor B. Once there, the life spirit of the occupants is drained by the drifting sirens; ships orbit endlessly, their desiccated crews never having known the final moment of death, so entranced were they by the songs of the Kiiry being transmitted through the subspace crystals of their communications controls. The space around Ivixor B, thus, has become a Sargasso Sea of wrecks, through which the Kiiry swim in lazy, almost innocent abandon. Why they are destructive is not known; and what they achieve by the indolent killing of other races has never been divined.

The Fire Bugs of Paludron IV

One of the most unusual life forms in the Oisir-Raxxla Sector is the race of semi-sentient creatures called the Eotarx. Paludron IV is a hostile world, not large,

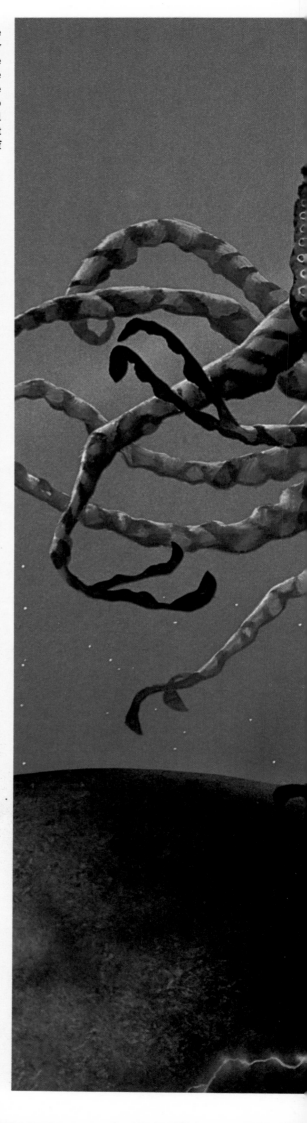

Previous page: Deathframe of Ahmed Samarandara, the great human explorer who gave his name to so many of the Universe's wonders, including the Samarandara Pearls. Right: The sirens of Ivixor B, more commonly known as the Kiiry. They are giant, medusoid creatures, which swim in the upper atmosphere of their violent and uninhabitable world. In the medusoid form the Kiiry are non-hostile and manifest a benign and advanced intelligence. Unfortunately when the Kiiry mature they transform into interplanetary organisms that seem incapable of relating to any other race save by killing it.

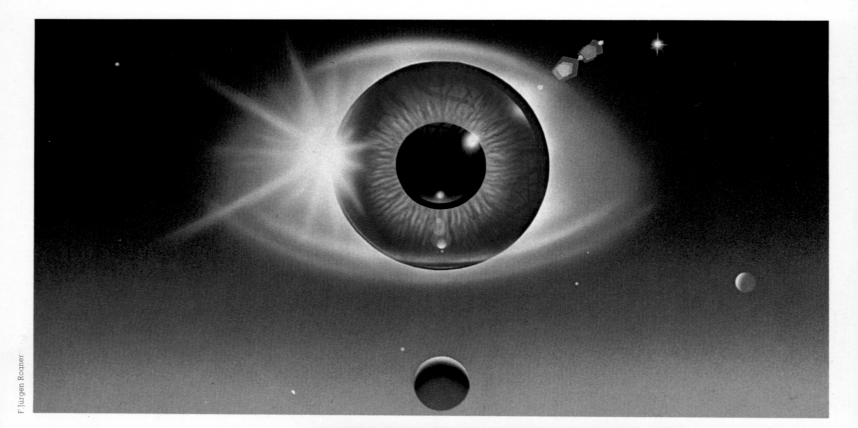

F Jurgen Rogner

David Hardy

Edward Blair Wilkins

but very young, with a thin crust and a reputation of being the most volcanic world in the Universe (which it is not). The Eotarx are leathery creatures, with wings and asbestos-like skins. They live in cliffs and on the steep slopes of some of the larger volcanoes, riding the whorls of boiling air, often as high as the stratosphere itself. They hunt smaller winged creatures and use their long, steely jaws to tear open the rocky substrate, reaching down to the warm rock beneath where all manner of juicy creatures live in burrows and cracks. Since the Eotarx have manipulable hands on their wings and can fashion tools out of stone and solidifying metals, they are thought to possess a limited measure of intelligence. Certainly, their rocky eyries are made from dressed stone and feature hand-carved supporting arches, designed to maximize the size and safety of the cavernous halls in which the communities live.

What is unusual about the Eotarx, however, is not their blossoming intelligence, but their fire death ritual. The Oisir-Raxxla, who have monitored this life form for thousands of years, call this *raarkar-maki*, after the sound uttered by the Eotarx as they gather for the ritual. Raarkarmaki occurs every 100 years, the generation time of the Eotarx. From across the planet, the communities fly northward, to the ring of volcanoes that encircles the northern planetary axis. When thousands, even millions, of the reptilian Eotarx have gathered in the valleys and lava plains between the volcanoes, an enormous winged ascent occurs. Shoals of the creatures surge up into the high atmosphere, where their sheer numbers turn the sky blacker than the ash can ever make it. Then, in columns, squadrons of Eotarx dive into the volcanic fires, to be burned instantly to cinders. The smoke of their deaths billows purplish from the craters, spreading out to form a pall of indigo gloom across the

*Top: The Eye of the Beholder. A Raxxlan projection which appeared above the primitive world Winter D, populated by sentient, but unadvanced insectoids. The Eye became an overwhelming symbol of the evil that stared from the heavens, so disorienting the creatures that the Oisir-Raxxla were able to build their structure and depart without life being lost. **Above:** Kiiry in the adult and hostile form. Known as sirens, because of the sound they could emit on subspace levels, the Kiiry have become a major cause of lost life in Human explorations into the Raxxlan Zone. **Right:** The Samarandara Pearls, the home system of the Oisir-Raxxla, seen beyond one of their trading ships.*

whole planet. And for a Human century the world is deserted, the volcanoes quiet. Abruptly the planet explodes into volcanic activity, from pole to pole, right around the equatorial rim. The world literally burns as fire is spewed from the depths. Amidst that fire are hundreds and thousands of fire seeds, tiny embryonic

Eotarx that drift up into the high atmosphere and float there until they hatch. The fledglings, no bigger than a Terran sparrow, fly down to the volcanic fires where they find a mother creature basking in the molten rock. Here, protected by her from the heat, they feed and grow; when the mother is exhausted she expires.

DOMINANT INTELLIGENCES: HUMANKIND, AND
LIFE-FORMS (HUMANOID) MUTANT), SEC) INTELLIGENT
OF LIFE-FORMS, (43) (SIC) 1212 **. EARTH. YEARS
DOMINANCE 5000 [EZRAAD) 2000 ** NO. OF
CONTROLLED EZRAAD) 1693 LEZRAAD)
CONTROLLED 2216 [HUMAN CONTROLLED).

David Hardy

Above: An image from the Book of Chaak, *shows Oriathan ships attacking a Ranan Colony world. A Ranan defence vessel, disguised as natural landscape, rises to meet the offenders. This sort of skirmish seems to have gone on for many hundreds of years, necessitating the constant maintenance of borders between the various subdivisions of the Tholmathon Empire. When the Empire finally came back together it seems that our own Galaxy was chosen as the central Star World for the formation of a Peace Corps.* **Right:** *Merlaka the Silver, one of the Great Lords of the family Galaej, and a natural leader of the Tholmathon. This is Lord Merlaka as a youth, his form humanoid now, fighting a ritual duel against the son of one of the families of the Rana. According to Chaak, Merlaka defeated a thousand sons in single-handed combat.*

That part of Known Space bordered by the Night Wall, the Urgenirk Darks and Garamond's Rift, contains the birthplace of the Human race, and is known as the Human Sector. However, Humankind is not the only dominant, spacefaring species in this vast area of space, nor indeed do they have control over more than a small part of the Sector. Their main enemy is the Empire of Ezraaq, the so-called Witch Lords of Ezraaq who are committed to the task of confining the Humans to the galaxy of their origination. But the history of the Human Sector is not just a story of two empires, expanding and opposing each other. It is the story, too, of the Tholmathon, who were known as the Shining Ones to many of the worlds they overLorded and, millions of years on, are still remembered in many ancient legends. The Tholmathon are dead now, vanished from the Universe in form, though not in spirit. Theirs was the first

story of Universal exploration, theirs the first race in our part of the Universe to break free of the restrictions of relativity and leave their mark on other worlds.

The Tholmathon evolved on the once ocean-covered world of Marangora II, now an arid and dessicated planet, littered with the crystalline remains of the Shining Ones. A hundred million years ago it was a water world of violence and beauty, with a richness of life unparalleled in the Universe. From the plethora of swimming and oozing life forms came an amphibious creature that took advantage of the massive, richly vegetated mountain ranges that rose above the waters. The Tholmathon were born, capable of living in both environments, capable of exploiting both. Originally, they were gigantic creatures, multiple eyed, black skinned and sluggish. In time they evolved a smaller form and became sleek and fast. Other forms of life were leaving the seas and

Above: *Merlaka the Silver, without his silver robes. The Great Lord is seen for the amphibia-form that he is. What intrigues Humans is the 'prison-bowl' the Tholmathon Lord holds, for the trapped spirit within has been identified as the son of the great Ahmed Samarandara, who was lost whilst exploring the space zones of the Kiiry. Whether this is simply an astrophysical conceit on Merlaka's part, or whether the preserved spirit is used as some kind of dynamo is uncertain. In the background is the city of Shabazarak. now ruined. but reconstructed by human archaeologists.* **Right:** *Time Storm: the Book of Chaak contains many holo-projections, and stories, of the strange life forms. On the world we know as Dickson's World (Soligazarra XII), the Scientific Department of the Military Branch of the League of Oriath experimented with time. One of the results was a 'storm of time', Creatures were dragged into the Tholmathon present from a variety of future times of the world. The world would later be colonised by Earth, and the Human female suggests one explanation for the disappearance of so many Humans from this world. The primitive Human possibly represents a return to the primitive of the colonists of our own time. The leopard is presumably a pet. The figure in the background is obviously a Narathnu trader. The Narathnu merchants were generally thought to be under the misguided rule of the meglomaniac Con Orger, an almost hairless alien form.*

populating the steeply sloping continental lands, and the Tholmathon learned first to hunt them, then to herd them, and then to breed them. In their final form, the Tholmathon were not unlike upright, hairy toads: ugly, to be sure, yet benign, brilliant, and already fascinated by the stars, and the 'dreamvoices' they could detect from them.

The Tholmathon Story

The *Crystal Record*, also known as the *Book of Chaak*, discovered on the long dead world of Marangora II, makes it clear how quickly the Tholmathon developed from agricultural creatures into scientific beings of an incredibly sophisticated attitude: just 40 generations. The *Crystal Record* – which took 2000 years to translate – is a logging, as if by a crewman on board a patrol vessel, of the history, myths and explorations of the Tholmathon at the height of their power. It makes reference, a third of the way through, to a world of oceans, swampy lands and lush vegetation, where giant amphibians roamed, and all the signs pointed to the evolution of intelligence within a few hundred millennia. Tholmathon had visited Earth during the Permian, which gives an idea of the time that has elapsed between their height of glory, and ours. Perhaps they had anticipated that the dinosaurs would be the Great Life that they had detected in the gene pools of Earth. They were sadly mistaken. The Tholmathon were extinct before those reptilian giants came upon the Earth. It would have been a long wait for Humankind.

Interestingly, in the same part of the *Record* is an account of the expedition to contact the last outpost of colonists on Earth, called the Lajial: '. . . fugitives from the dying Sand World, themselves destined to extinction in the sterile cities that nestled among the violent life of the third world . . .'. No trace of those Martians, for surely the *Crystal Record* refers to creatures from that dead world, has ever been found, no artifact, no life, no memory. The martians had suffered the despair of climatic extinction so long ago that the face of their world has been changed a thousand times, obscuring all sign of them. Only a Tholmathon picture remains.

The Tholmathon spread through the galaxy, using a relativity-reducing drive that distorted time, but not space. They formed what the *Record* tells us was the First Empire of the Shining, and for the first time the ruling elite became known as the Shining Lords (or Kings: the meaning of the *Record* is difficult to decipher on this and many points). The Shining Lords were benign, but suffered from the problem common to all great empires – communication difficulties.

Without the thruspace concept of later scientific evolution, the First Empire, insufficiently policed, inevitably decayed into rebellion. The galaxy split into several warring factions, finding any excuse to send a warp drive fleet to the neighbouring Sectors: trade disagreement, political slight, kidnapping and so forth. This was a pattern to be repeated during the

31

First Federation of the Human Space Empire. For the Tholmathon it was disastrous. Within ten generations all that they had built in the way of colonial worlds and trade cooperation had collapsed into a barbaric mayhem. Four Federations of Worlds emerged. Two, the League of Oriath, and the Rana Federation, survived the squabbling to become powerful empires in their own right, keeping away from each other in the galaxy, but beginning the task of crossing intergalactic space. For now, at last, the Tholmathon had developed the thruspace drive, and could measure distance travelled in lEons, not just light years.

The Rana Federation explored outwards towards what we call the Kalpecca Star Shallows. They made contact with the life forms of what is now the Oisir-Raxxla Sector, although at that time there were no races of star-travelling capability. The Urgenirk Darks were considered less dangerous, less vast than they are now thought to be. The League of Oriath, led by its great family, the Galaej, expanded towards the Night Wall, and crossed the vast trench of empty space that is Garamond's Rift, into the deserted and virtually lifeless Uan-irec Sector. It was the League that documented Sol and her several worlds, and who recorded for posterity the dying Martians.

Soon the League of Oriath, the confederation of ten great families led by the StarMaster of the Galaej, formed itself into an empire, the Second Empire. Tired of looking outward beyond the starless rifts, the Empire looked back, towards the Star Shallows where the ruthless and despotic Rana Empire ruled the hundreds of colonized worlds of the southern Sector.

War was inevitable, and a stalemate more so. The great kings of each Empire fought a hundred worlds for the possession of a million. Eventually an uneasy peace was declared. This was in the time of the Seventh Family of Galaej, led by a king called Merlaka the Silver, already at the end of his life. Merlaka lived in a glitteringly huge crystal castle on the perfect world of Vizna, an early colony world at the heart of the League of Oriath. Among his thousands of offspring he had long since designated the three who would contest the Rulership after his death, a ritual that had long been practised by the Tholmathon. In the years before the contest could occur, however, the male heirs, warriors all, had become troublesome, squabbling among themselves, and seeking favours among the other Galaej. Each had been confined to a galactic zone of his own, to rule as minor god until the call came for them to attend upon Vizna. But the eldest, who was the first bred in the body of the Empress of the Galaej, escaped the galaxy with his fleet of warships and befriended the unstable and power-hungry youngest offspring of the Lord of the Rana. With their space fleets united, and their determination to jointly rule the Universe undeterred by the needs of Tholmathon honour and ritual, they systematically killed the sibling heirs of the Oriath League, and turned against

Above: Within Ezraaq dominated space several intelligent species coexist, all of them trying to achieve an independence from the magic-wielding overseers; one of these, and perhaps the most difficult for man to relate to, is the Thooryx. The Thooryx are vast, ameoboidal creatures, a cross between gigantic, space-drifting slugs, and shapeless amoebas. They usually squeeze their protoplasmic bulk into Humanoid-shaped metal suits in order to communicate with sensitive species such as our own. Right: Ezraaq magic platforms: Warrior-wizards ride solo platforms through space, powered by energy-spells, and packed with military equipment.

Vizna.

The *Crystal Record* is incomplete as to what occurred, save that the impetuous youths were destroyed, and their armies with them. Although the League and the Federation remained in existence for 1000 years or more, and exploration and trade with emerging worlds continued, it is clear that the interruption of the Shining Life, the sacred family line that was such a stable factor in the League, was too much to bear, and the Oriath collapsed. They withdrew to a handful of colony worlds, where they remain today, a primitive race of beings known as the Dithon. They have evolved many different forms, as have the sad remnants of the Ranans. They carry no memory of their great past. In truth, they are not the true descendants of those glorious Empires, merely distant shadows.

The Ezraaq Witch Lords

Long after the Tholmathon had declined, leaving the Universe practically bare of any spacefaring race, the Ezraaq evolved on the giant, but hollow world of Jadrax IV, first called 'Big Planet' by Human ex-

plorers. The size of Sol's Jupiter, the world has no more mass than Earth, and a very low gravity. Its centre is honeycombed almost to nothingness. Within that centre, save for the very core where the heat still existed, a vast variety of life forms battled with each other for supremacy. Our lemur-like ancestors were foraging on the plains of Africa when the Ezraaq evolved their first intelligent forms. A million Earth years passed, and on Earth itself little evolution occurred; but in that time the Ezraaq found the secrets of time and space and spread out through the Universe.

They have – and had then – two peculiarities, one of which remains the reason for their success and makes them the terrifying and near-invincible enemy that they are, the other an anatomical peculiarity that led, some millennia ago, to the substantial reduction of their power.

The Ezraaq are tall, angular, rather bird-like creatures, with atrophied wings, which they can nevertheless still extend into wide, coloured back fans. The males have strange, wing-like structures on their heads. The most unusual biological feature of the Ezraaq is the number of their

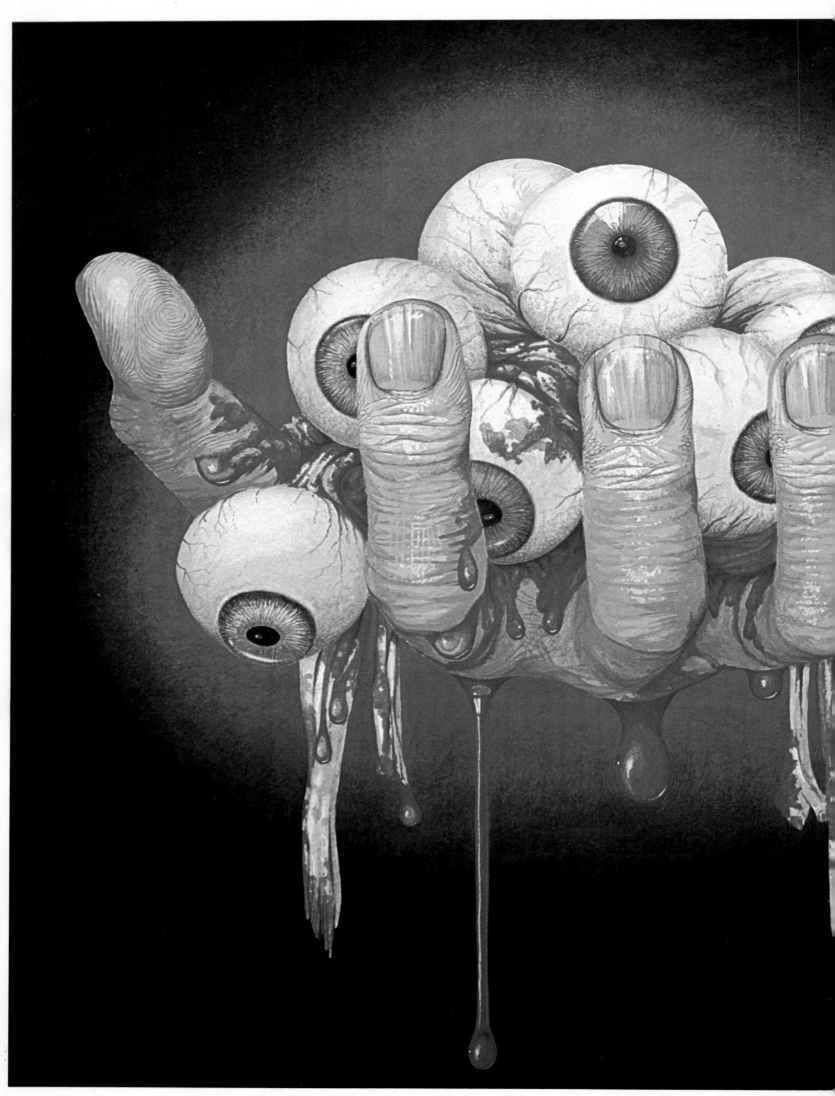

Left: One of the more gory, and yet very effective, of the Ezraaq spell-weapons is this interspatial projection of images that are particularly repulsive to the Human mind. Eyeballs dripping blood, disembowelled bodies, gigantic insects are all made to move to give them an appearance of fascinating reality. This picture was taken from the bridge of a Human minesweeper, equipped with the new Systemic-shock Override Control. The ship senses the terror and disgust in its Human crew and immediately assuming battlestations and control itself. *Above:* Tyrranak. Not the best depiction of these intelligent creatures. The Ezraaq artist had obviously attempted to portray the tyrranak in its primitive form to denigrate their degree of achievement. Tyrranak is the Human name for these impressively ugly reptilioids. With their thick legs and vestigial forelimbs, they are reminiscent of the thunder lizards of Earth's first cretuceous period, but have a far greater intelligence.

sexes: they have three. Of the thousands of intelligent and potentially-intelligent life forms in the Universe, only a handful have more than two sexes, although many hundreds are unisexual or hermaphrodite.

Incidentally, the record for sexual number is held in the Human Sector, and belongs to the elephantine Hunga of the heavy planet Zer Verref VII. The Hunga have 29 sexes, each supplying one 'chromosome' to the final gamete, although chromosome hardly describes the complex organic molecule that is used for passing genetic information in the Hunga. Partially intelligent, the Hunga have now reduced the generation time of their species from 11000 to 1000 years; the task of getting all the sexes together was one of the reasons for their evolutionary backwardness, especially as they were solitary rather than herd creatures. Now they organize regular gatherings and dance and mate beneath the full light of Zer Verref's seven moons.

The three sexes of the Ezraaq are male, female and carrier. The three forms are quite distinct, the carrier being quite unlike the male and female. It is shorter, and less able to defend itself, but in the animalistic phase of Ezraaq evolution, was fleet footed and foul tasting, and was therefore able to survive where the other sexes might perish.

Male and female gametes are implanted by an ordinary sexual process, in the common womb of the carrier, where fertilization occurs not of one, but of hundreds of the larger gametes from the male. The function of the carrier is to incubate these tiny embryos, rejecting those which show faults or bad survival characteristics. Towards the end of gestation, a vicious battle is fought *in utero*. The clawed young methodically eliminate each other until only one of each sex remains. When they reach term, the young gouge their way into the specially toughened alimentary canal of the carrier and burst out of the lower of its two mouths. After birth, the sexual roles are familiar: the female suckles the young, the male trains them in survival behaviour, the carrier awaits the next breeding season.

This intriguing biological peculiarity is often forgotten, however, since the Ezraaq have one of the strangest and most fascinating technologies imaginable. Their world, Jadrax IV, apparently exists in a part of space where there is *velaqua tension* in the quark stratum matrix. This is a phenomenon well known to Human scientists – the planet Uranus in the Solar System passes through such a region of space every 1200 years – but it is not something they have ever managed to fully understand. It is likely that the Ezraaq have no real understanding of the phenomenon either, they only know the effect. Normal scientific principles do not apply on Jadrax IV. Rather, a peculiar, almost abnormal response to physical properties is experienced: metals transmute through the periodic table; structure changes as if in the winking of a visual organ. The word for this phenomenon used to be magic. Now it is called 'matrix tension scientific mislocation'. The Ezraaq, knowing no different, have of course made the best of their technology of magic and spells. They are as baffled by conventional science as is the Human Empire by a space fleet that is propelled by a 'spell', and which finds its laser swords deflected by a bolt of 'magic force'.

The great technological breakthrough for the Ezraaq was the discovery, by white magicians, of the time spell, the combination of incantations and patterns that could cause the flux of time to change within the area of a material body, such as a space ship. The scientific equivalent would be the time phase aspect of the thru-space drive. When the Ezraaq evolved the natural formula – a distillation of plant and ground rock substrate which, when ingested and accompanied by the limb movements of the 'forward pass', enabled a material body to move at superlight velocities – their spacefaring began. They have 40 different weapons spells, mostly 'effect' spells, that is, the changing of the environment around the enemy. They have developed fire power, some of it fire power as Humans understand it. (It must be remembered that away from the peculiar homeworld of Jadrax, they encounter normal physical phenomena, even though their evolved magic powers remain intact.) Much of the technology they use is simple parascience, or psionic radiation. This is a physicochemical attribute of all bioelectric systems, such as the brain, which is heightened in areas of space where time is 'tense'. Humans have a very limited psychic ability, related to the fact that the Earth is tugged by the dual gravities of its sun and a large moon; this has a slight effect upon the time field around the planet.

The Ezraaq Empire came to dominate the galaxy of its birth in about the year 10000 BE. Not until the year 3000 AE, when the Humans were already rapidly spreading to fill their own galaxy did the Ezraaq breach intergalactic space. Their First Empire under the rule of Hegethark Nightsword, the Supreme Wizard, rapidly spread out along the edge of Garamond's Rift, and towards the Tharana Void, establishing colonies and vast floating cities at the heart of each galaxy. Within a matter of a few hundred years, they entered the rings of the Human galaxy, and here for the first time they met a spacefaring race as obsessed with weapons technology as themselves. The first skirmish, the battle of the Dorngest Star Ridge, was more an exchange of confusion than fire; but thereafter Human and Ezraaq battled constantly at the rim and in the globular clusters of the galaxy for domination. The Ezraaq were finally defeated by the full force of the Galactic Federation, a Human space fleet drawn from 1000 independent worlds.

Above: Garathaan Shield of Night, a great Ezraaq Lord. The two million inhabited worlds of the Ezraaq Sector are now under the control of the most benign of the Ezraaq Wizards, Garathaan. He has established a more friendly, and co-operative contact with the Federation of Terran Star Cities, and the other planetary groups within the Human Sector. Here he is transformed into semi-human shape, riding a smaller version of the magic platform. **Right:** *Ezraaq floating city. The first Empire of the Ezraaq, under the rule of Hegethark Nightsword, rapidly spread out from the home Galaxy, along the edge of Garamond's Rift, and towards the Tharana Void. As it moved it established colonies peopled from these vast floating cities, many of which still remain in orbit about the colonised worlds. The cities were the first great technological achievements of the Ezraaq, able to carry five million of their kind to the outposts of their Empire.*

Thereafter, the Ezraaq withdrew and agreed an uneasy peace. Human technologists, not slow to study the Ezraaq techniques of space and war, were able to interpret the 'magic' drive, if not exactly copy it. By the year 4288 AE, the Humans were in intergalactic space, exploring the Sector away from the Ezraaq Empire. The

Treaty of Kalpecca, 5623 AE, defined Ezraaq Space and Human Space, leaving the bulk of the Sector for free trade and without overLordship. Naturally, this treaty was abused time and again, and the war with the Ezraaq has been a long, fluctuating and tedious one.

The Ezraaq Empire now consists of

11000 galaxies and some two million inhabited worlds, the Ezraaq, with their carrier sex, being able to colonize practically any world providing it can cater for their basic needs. These worlds are under the aegis of the most benign of the Ezraaq Wizards, Garathaan Shield of Night, who has established more friendly contact with the Federation of Terran Star Cities and the Human Space League of Worlds. Already Garathaan grows old, however, and his quartet of offspring war and squabble about the succession, and who shall lead the first fleet against the Human Frontier Worlds.

Within the Ezraaq Section of the Universe, three intelligent species coexist. Dominated by the Ezraaq, they are nonetheless manifestly unhappy with the situation, and are threatened with extermination should their protests for independence become much louder.

The Thooryx are vast amoeboid creatures, without anatomical skeletal material, who confine themselves within metal suits in order to present a familiar appearance to the predominantly humanoid controllers of the galaxy. The Tyrranak, which is the Human name for these impressively ugly reptiles, with thick legs and rather vestigal forelimbs, are reminiscent of the thunder lizard of

The Human form: To an Ezraaq this must represent the most familiar view of the Human Species. A proud, bipedal, warrior, shooting to kill before the Ezraaq's magic can turn his weapon into stone. This trooper is dressed in the Skirmish kit of a Malaccan Marauder, an elite group of highly trained soldiers who prowl the border zone between Human and Ezraaq space, and prevent the passage of solitary wizards wherever they can. They style themselves Waynesmen after a legendary Earth hero of the early Space Age.

Michael Whelan

Left: Human diplomatic group on Andaluce. Andaluce (Antarres III) has become an administrative centre of the Galactic League, and like the famous Nuxor is a world that has become practically a single city; open spaces remain, such as this park with patches of real grass. **Above:** Orenians snatched from the clutches of an Ezraaq wizard. The Ezraaq regard the tiny Orenians as something of a joke, and use them extensively for magic experimentation. This group includes the great Orenian writer Ch'chak-chik. They are being led to safety by a skirmisher who has 'frozen' the wizard's spell upon him, keeping him in the form of a boar.

Earth's Cretaceous period. The Tyrranak enjoy an ordered society, fashioned over the millenia from their solitary animal behaviour; but the society is unstable, with murder and ritual attack being the commonest crimes as old attitudes continually surface. However, they have developed the beginnings of a space drive, and have colonized two of the three moons of their world. Finally, there are the Orenians, small, black-skinned humanoids, almost totally featureless save for their single eyes. The tallest Orenian stands about 30 centimetres. They are a matriarchal society, and the male population appears to be subdivided into an intellectual elite, and a drone-like majority, whose lifespan is very artificially reduced every Orenian year. Emissaries from Orenia have visited Earth to request help in fighting the Ezraaq, who seem to treat these tiny beings as something of a joke and use their world to practise various advanced forms of magic research, with the drones as guinea pigs.

The Human Zone

The Human race effectively polices, and

trades with, the galaxies between its own Star City and the Null Zone that separates the Human Sector from the Kalpecca Star Shallows. This is a vast area of the Sector, and includes more than 1100 planetary life forms known, collectively, as the Dithon, the direct descendants of the extinct Tholmathon. It also includes a number of intelligent alien forms, and several hundred life forms that show the first signs of a development beyond the critical MFE factor of 10, at which level they will be capable of developing fusion power. All of these creatures are left strictly alone. The Laws of NonInterference are respected, on the whole, by military and trader ships alike, although there are instances when such ships break the law by either landing or being seen. It is the expressed wish of the Government of Earth that all developing species be allowed to find space in their own way and in their own time; but of course, the Vegan Treaty and Agreement of Space Protection laid down in 6772 AE, means that whenever Ezraaq warships penetrate the Human Sector, and make planetfall, the Human military must respond. Thus, among the developing worlds there are species who are now cognizant of the existence of 'aliens', and whose cultures have thus changed.

The history of Human expansion into space is complex. The continual technological reversions caused by war, the Solar Flares of 897 AE, which had such a disastrous effect on Human culture, and the assumption of power by the Religious Army of the Americas in 1472 AE which stopped all exploration of the stars for a hundred years, brought to an end the First Stellar Age. The basic history begins with the landing of the *Eagle* in the year zero. Then followed 400 years of solar exploration, during which the Human race established scientific communities on four satellites and two worlds of the planetary system of their sun. With the vast mineral resources now available, Human energy problems ended. It is from this moment onward that the correct balance between leisure and technological advancement was gradually achieved. Despite the setbacks of political war, the achievement of thruspace came quickly. The First Stellar Age was short lived, to be sure, but the religious fervour of the Holy Rule – invoking the resurrection of the dead who, it was felt, should all be on the Mother World – soon passed away. The Second Stellar Age reestablished contact with the isolated colonies of the galaxy, many of whom now claimed their independence and who had developed a sufficiently different weapons technology to bring force to their argument. Thus the League of Worlds was established, which led ultimately to the First Federation.

As Humankind spread into the Universe, they became well aware of the Ezraaq threat. Struggling to develop their own space drive to the ultimate sophisticated level, they suffered many setbacks at the hands of the magicians before the Treaty of Separation was at last written down in 5587 AE, leading to the Treaty of Kalpecca a few years later.

Thereafter, the several Leagues of Worlds were fused to form the Galactic League, with an administrative centre on Andaluce (Antarres III) a world that, like Nuxor and Trantor, had become a single city. Ruling families, religious leaders, empires, kingships, all of these things existed somewhere within the Human Sector, but all agreed that their worlds and their resources, belonged to the Greater Cause of Humankind. Trading empires, it must be said, continually abused the Principle of One Ownership – whereby each Human individual has the right to claim that they own a fraction of a part of everything and therefore cannot be denied access to space – leading to skirmishes, downfalls, and a change in power structure. However, the League of Ships, the fleet under control of the United Galaxies, is so powerful now, that when used against even an empire, it can win by a show of power, rather than actual battle.

The Cryogods of Thangenna II

What, then, of the intelligent species that find themselves within the Human Sector of space? Among the Dithon, one world

Above: Forms of the Dithon, the scattered remnants of the great Tholmathon. This group from several worlds, is a diplomatic team visiting one of the Human colony worlds and enjoying one of the Human luxuries that is always made available on the far flung empire worlds — real terrestrial ice cream. Right: Track's World, the home of the Panatagruthal, a Humanoid race monitored by the Human League. League Medical Law forbids us to show the Panatagruthal themselves, since their appearance — they are covered with a hideous fungal parasite — is offensive and disgusting. They skulk in a jungle world which is a place of great beauty, ironically. Skip ships patrol it, but permanent settlement is extremely unlikely. This is a shame, since the world is ideal for colonization.

has begun the process of recovery. After millions of years of existence upon a world where once they were 'seeded', the garDithon on the frozen world of Thangenna II, have adapted perfectly to the snow and ice, and all-year-round temperatures that approach the freezing point of oxygen. The garDithon have developed double skins. They are huge creatures, sluggish, yet with machine power and a refined religion. The difficulty that presents itself to other species making contact with the garDithon is that an ancient race memory of the Tholmathon, their travelling and ownership of so much of the Universe, has given the garDithon an inverted sense of godhead: instead of creating a god to explain life, they believe that they themselves are god, and all life has been created by them. This amusing arrogance is, in fact, intolerable when confronted, for they find the Human race exceptionally ugly and offensive and have no qualms about 'eliminating one of Their less successful works of creation'.

The Symbiotes on Entiba IV

The Panatagruthal, a thin, transparent-skinned humanoid species living in the steamy jungles of Track's World (Entiba IV), caused something of an embarrassment for the ever-humane kingship of New Britain, one of the smaller galaxies in

the Human Sector, where a Royal Family has been in existence for four millennia. The Panatagruthal are one of several alien species overseen, out of sight, by the Human military of New Britain. Early on, it was noticed that the humanoids were infested with the most hideous skin disease, a repulsive, expanding, dark fungal growth, that began at the extremities of hands and feet (the Panatagruthal have two pairs of arms) and spread to envelop the whole body, including the head, at which time a significant behavioural change occurred, although the humanoids did not die. A surreptitious medical team isolated a small community of Panatagruthal in an attempt to cure them of the disease. To their horror – and bemusement – they discovered that the humanoids were unintelligent hunting animals in a symbiotic relationship with the fungus. The fungus was intelligent, and communicated through its host. Track's World is now left in total isolation, although a team of anthropologists is believed to be established somewhere on the planet, learning the fungal-Panatagruthal's traditions and memories.

The Jelly Babies of Chorepsis VIII

The Luraliv, of the water world Chorepsis VIII (which is in the original Human galaxy, although it was not discovered

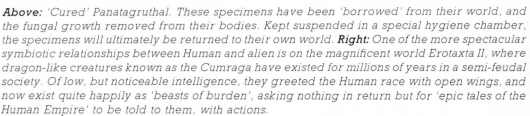

Above: *'Cured' Panatagruthal. These specimens have been 'borrowed' from their world, and the fungal growth removed from their bodies. Kept suspended in a special hygiene chamber, the specimens will ultimately be returned to their own world.* *Right:* *One of the more spectacular symbiotic relationships between Human and alien is on the magnificent world Erotaxta II, where dragon-like creatures known as the Cumraga have existed for millions of years in a semi-feudal society. Of low, but noticeable intelligence, they greeted the Human race with open wings, and now exist quite happily as 'beasts of burden', asking nothing in return but for 'epic tales of the Human Empire' to be told to them, with actions.*

until the seventh millennium AE), are single-sexed creatures with a bizarre reproductive method and a highly developed intellectual ability, although in machine technology terms they are very primitive. The Luraliv are most familiarly described as jelloid, although their shape is vaguely Human. They walk upright, have a slight pigmentation of the skin and eyes, sense organs set in a head, and flexible fingers at the end of their limbs. They are extremely friendly, and glad of the contact with the Human Empire. Although the adult Luraliv spend much of their time on the rocky, rather sparsely vegetated land masses, they are dependent on water, and frequently return to the deep oceans for various rituals. Each

Luraliv is both male and female, but they can modify their own genetic structure to accommodate violent climatic changes, or to take advantage of speed, low energy production or such like. Fertilization occurs internally, and the Luraliv literally begins to grow a second body. This body shows through one or other of its sides, growing at right angles. A second offspring is triggered to balance the first; each offspring itself divides, the main body of the Luraliv growing larger and stronger, to support the weight. When some 30 individuals are budding, the adult appears as an immense mass of jelloid heads and waving arms, and in this condition it returns to the sea where the development continues to completion.

45

DOMINANT INTELLIGENCE: ORGANIC, SINGLE AUHANOID
GESTALT MIND, ORIG. TINY EXOSKELETAL CREEP.
INTELLIGENT LIFE FORMS: 4 MILLION, LIFE ON
ANDALUCEI* EARTH YEARS OF DOMINANCE: UNKNOWN
NO. OF GALAXIES: 38,000

RECORDS ON

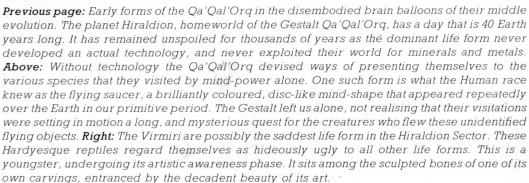

Previous page: Early forms of the Qa'Qal'Orq in the disembodied brain balloons of their middle evolution. The planet Hiraldion, homeworld of the Gestalt Qa'Qal'Orq, has a day that is 40 Earth years long. It has remained unspoiled for thousands of years as the dominant life form never developed an actual technology, and never exploited their world for minerals and metals.
Above: *Without technology the Qa'Qal'Orq devised ways of presenting themselves to the various species that they visited by mind-power alone. One such form is what the Human race knew as the flying saucer, a brilliantly coloured, disc-like mind-shape that appeared repeatedly over the Earth in our primitive period. The Gestalt left us alone, not realising that their visitations were setting in motion a long, and mysterious quest for the creatures who flew these unidentified flying objects.* ***Right:*** *The Virmiri are possibly the saddest life form in the Hiraldion Sector. These Hardyesque reptiles regard themselves as hideously ugly to all other life forms. This is a youngster, undergoing its artistic awareness phase. It sits among the sculpted bones of one of its own carvings, entranced by the decadent beauty of its art.*

That part of the Known Universe referred to as the Hiraldion Sector lies far beyond the Night Wall, and is the most inaccessible. Although very far from Human-occupied space, Human traffic into this Sector has been encouraged by the presiding intelligences. The Sector comprises some 30000 galaxies, a large proportion of which are globular and T-shaped, formations incomprehensible to the early astronomers. Among these galaxies approximately four million worlds are believed to be inhabited by intelligent life, mostly the descendants of the early days of exploration by the various dominant life species in the Sector.

The dominant life form in the Hiraldion Sector in the eleventh millennium is the Qa'Qal'Orq, a race of beings who long ago fused their individual minds into one

single entity, or gestalt. Their early history on Hiraldion, their homeworld, was uneventful. They were always a passive, contemplative race who preferred thought to action. They suffered no wars or revolutions during their progress to maturity, and lived in total harmony with the lower life forms on Hiraldion. The planet thus remained unspoiled and unexploited, and can be seen to be so to this day.

Although the Qa'Qal'Orq were not the first intelligent beings to evolve in their Sector of the Universe, when they began to explore their own galaxy, using an early technology based on time and space warp, they soon discovered that no life existed elsewhere within their small Star City. Alone in their own galaxy, and unable to cover the distances to galaxies

elsewhere, they withdrew to Hiraldion in some distress, and abandoned their technology to concentrate on developing their minds.

The Qa'Qal'Orq were a humanoid race, and as generation succeeded generation they found that their heads were growing larger at the expense of their bodies. So steeped did they become in contemplative thought that they eventually found their bodies to be a hindrance and dispensed with them altogether. For a while they resembled immense, gas-filled balloons, the modified skulls drifting on the winds, powered by the small brain unit that rested on the lower inside surface. Soon all material form was abandoned. They became beings of pure mental energy who absorbed light directly from the sun into almost invisible energy systems in order to

sustain themselves.

At this stage of their evolution, each individual could only be seen as a glowing point of light, communicating telepathically with its fellow beings. The emotional state of each entity was determined from its prevailing colour: for example, pink indicated affection, yellow signified joy, and pale blue, excitement. During the long Hiraldion night (40 Human years) they became dormant, a state approximating to the hibernation of some Terran animals; but by day they were ceaselessly active in their quest for knowledge and a deeper understanding of the Universe.

After a time the single entities began to fuse together, combining their minds in order to reach greater levels of awareness and comprehension. Soon, this process reached its logical conclusion. Every

mentality was joined together to form a unified World Mind of awesome intellectual power; the Gestalt. The Qa'Qal'Orq Gestalt can be regarded as a single being, or as an assemblage of individual minds, but displays the characteristics of both. It is perhaps best understood as a colony of minds similar to an insect community, in which each individual works for the benefit of the whole. Their 'purpose' is to contemplate the Universe and to seek an increasingly sophisticated understanding of its mysteries.

Shortly after the Qa'Qal'Orq Gestalt had been formed, the sun about which their homeworld revolved, began to redden and grow dim, its supply of nuclear fuel exhausting itself through a tiny hole in space. The Qa'Qal'Orq did not want to abandon Hiraldion for another planet, for

it was still a beautiful world. So they brought their prodigious mental powers to bear and channelled interstellar hydrogen into the sun, rekindling it and securing their future on Hiraldion.

The Virmiri: Despondent Reptiles

The Qa'Qal'Orq had become a solitary, insular race during their long period of evolution. By the time the Gestalt was formed, other races had sprung up elsewhere, and indeed within their own galaxy. For many thousands of years no attempt was made to contact them. It may seem strange, therefore, that the Qa'Qal'Orq came to dominate their Sector of the Universe, but it must be remembered that during their gradual evolution towards the Gestalt, other races were well aware of the existence of the Qa'Qal'Orq.

Indeed, they were regarded as an enigma and as a challenge to the intellectual powers of communication. One such race were the Virmiri, from the world of Byorx, a young, technologically sophisticated race of beings who had long been embarked on a fruitless search for the legendary world, Xanjust. The Virmiri, more than any other race, were responsible for bringing the Qa'Qal'Orq out of their self-enforced isolation.

Byorx is a hot, swampy planet and the Virmiri are a bold and industrious reptilian race who developed from a primitive society into an advanced, spacefaring race in a remarkably short time (less than five millennia). Yet despite the sophistication of their society, the Virmiri were a tormented people. They considered themselves to be hideously ugly among

the races of the Universe, and their major religion taught them that they were all worthless, despicable beings who could find redemption only in death, when their souls would be transported to the world of Xanjust. There they would live a peaceful, harmonious existence for all eternity, inhabiting new bodies far finer and more beautiful than their reptilian forms.

When the Virmiri developed their interstellar drive they began to comb the galaxies for Xanjust. Their probeships discovered many inhabited worlds, but none were the paradise planet they sought. They grew increasingly disconsolate. Their continued failure to find Xanjust sank them even further in self-contempt. Then, during the reign of the Empress Roxacefienne of the Fifth Virmirion Federation, one of their probe-

ships came upon Hiraldion and discovered the Qa'Qal'Orq Gestalt, an immense web of multicoloured light draped over the equator of the lush and verdant planet.

The Qa'Qal'Orq had spent countless eons in their disembodied state and had long forgotten what it was like to inhabit a physical form. They sent mental tendrils into the minds of the Virmiri probeship crew and felt again the wind on their faces, the pressure of rock beneath their feet, the warmth of the sun. They saw their homeworld through Virmiri eyes, smelled the fragrance of the summer flowers now in bloom. They listened to the sounds of the animal life of the planet. All of these things they found wonderfully exciting. The only thing that disturbed them was the thoughts of the Virmiri themselves, steeped in the

despair and loathing characteristic of their race. The Qa'Qal'Orq, with their prodigious knowledge and wisdom, immediately understood why they felt this way and quickly banished these thoughts, replacing them with feelings of self respect and hope. The effect on the Virmiri crew was immediate. Freed at last from their burden of ignominy, they returned to Byorx to give their people the good news. Immediately Virmiri pilgrims began flocking to Hiraldion, there to be released from self torment by the benign wisdom of the Qa'Qal'Orq. The Virmiri was transformed as a result into the friendly, widespread race they are today. Braced with their new pride and purpose, the Virmiri became ambassadors for the Qa'Qal'Orq, bringing other sentient races to Hiraldion to draw on the Gestalt's deep store of

*Above: Adult Virmiri. This shows just how repulsive this gentle, and unloved, life form truly is. The adult male spends much time in water guarding the underwater 'brood pens' that have been filled by the female. Although they have the most negative ego in all the galaxies, the Virmiri still feel the need to reproduce. **Left:** A vision of the fabulous planet Xanjust, a Virmiri starship settling on its lush fields. This is the goal of the Virmiri quest, which has obsessed them for generations. Long ago, when their painful malaise of self-loathing and disgust set in, a myth grew up that somewhere in the Sector was a world where such creatures as the Virmiri could be transformed into beautiful and pleasant animals. An artist painted this interpretation of golden Xanjust, a Virmiri scout ship settling to land on its lush fields.*

empathy and understanding.

Many other species visited Hiraldion, which soon became the most revered planet in the Sector. The Bierbeirb of Zimrithin, giant, amorphous creatures, up to 13 kilometres across, inhabited a volcanic world and breathed the sulphurous gases of its atmosphere; but Zimrithin's volcanoes were slowly becoming extinct and the Bierbeirb was threatened with

asphyxiation by an overabundance of oxygen. The Qa'Qal'Orq deflected a great comet into orbit about Zimrithin, creating tidal stresses on the planet's crust which caused the extinct volcanoes to erupt once more and replenish the atmosphere.

The Urgaanatha were an advanced, slug-like telepathic race who feared open spaces. They had long lived deep underground in huge caverns on their home-

51

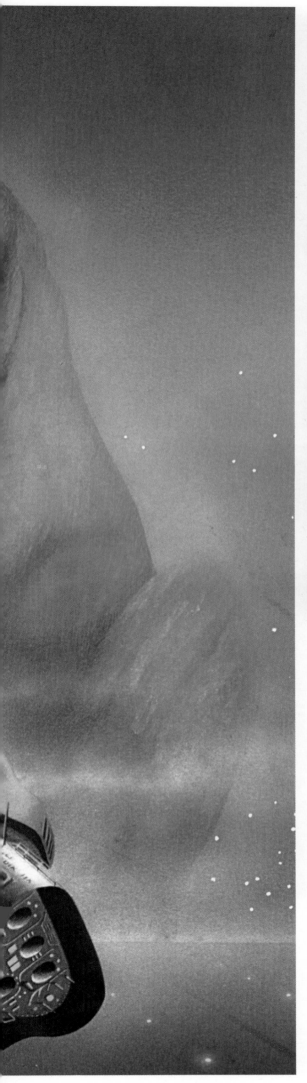

Left: The Ticireig, a proud and obstinate race, classified as tricephalic caninoform (three-headed dogs) and often referred to as Cerberands. The Ticireig are not naturally warlike, they just like to get their own way. *Above:* Half machine, half Humanoid, the Ragass are strange intelligences of the fire-covered world Renefa IV. They turned to the Gestalt for help in cooling the volcanic activity of their world. The Ragass do not appear to have a very high intelligence, and certainly seem incapable of having built the machine technology with which they are so closely linked. The Gestalt believe that, at some period in the distant past, another culture experimented with bionic machines, and Renefa IV has been the dumping ground for their failures. The Human race is suspected.

world, Tharian. They were unaware of intelligent life elsewhere until the Qa'Qal'Orq detected their telepathic emissions and dispatched a Virmiri probe-ship to make contact with them and to invite them to visit Hiraldion. The Qa'Qal'Orq cured them of their agora-phobia, and as a token of their gratitude the Urgaanatha made available to other species a compound crystallized from one of their subterranean rivers which showed miraculous healing properties against a great many diseases. Today, the main trade contact between the Human and Hiraldion Sectors is based on these crystals.

The Oetrenl of the world Paluberia are an intensely, almost pathologically, super-stitious race. For generations, they shied away from all contact with other species. Within recent history the Qa'Qal'Orq sent

a Virmiri observer ship to their planet. They discovered that Paluberia had a retinue of moons whose complex patterns in the sky were used by Oetrenl as-trologers to determine their people's be-haviour. When this fact was reported to the Qa'Qal'Orq, the Gestalt used its for-midable mental powers to alter the orbits of the moons in such a way as to arrange for a supremely favourable conjunction on the very day that a delegation arrived on Paluberia to negotiate the Oetrenl's entry into the Concordat of Worlds, which the Qa'Qal'Orq were establishing in the Hiraldion Sector. For the Oetrenl their arrival was so auspicious that they im-mediately accepted the delegation's pro-posals and joined the Concordat, thus breaking their isolation. The danger re-mains, however, and is often acute; the lives of the Oetrenl are totally governed

Oliviero Berni

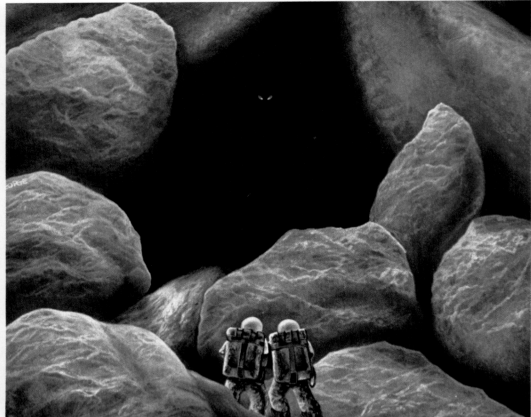

George Jones

by belief in the Cosmic Hand of God, who moves stars and moons in their courses, and makes winds blow to indicate his anger. Delegations from other worlds may be ecstatically welcomed, because the Star Omens are good, and then abruptly killed, simply because the pattern of clouds breaks up.

The only serious challenge to the Qa'Qal'Orq's attempt to establish the Concordat in the Hiraldion Sector came from the Yarrassad Federation. This was made up of four different species who inhabited worlds in a single globular cluster. Since each of the four worlds was close to the others, ties were strong and interference was resented. The dominant race, the Ticireig, were a proud, suspicious people who greatly benefited from the trading arrangements which they had established with their neighbours. Their planet, Lonmetris, was rich in the heavy metals vital to the other three worlds, if they were to sustain their technological development. The Ticireig feared that joining the Gestalt's Concordat would deprive them of their primacy. The Qa'Qal'Orq's overtures to the Federation were continually rebuffed, the Ticireig threatening war unless the Federation's independence was guaranteed. However, the three other worlds were less hostile, and the Qa'Qal'Orq arranged for supernova remnants to be deposited near their respective homeworlds, ensuring them of an independent supply of heavy metals. The Ticireig were now in an impossible position and were forced to join the Concordat. In an attempt to restore their pride, the Qa'Qal'Orq invited them to supply one of the three delegates from the Hiraldion Concordat to the Shillath Conference, on the central world of Shillath where trade agreements between the various zones of the Hiraldion Sector

Top left: *The Urganaatha are an advanced, slug-like, telepathic race who have a mortal fear of open spaces. Many of them live in the depths of the oceans, especially adapted to the pressure. Here, a Gestalt presence in the body of a Simnimarian, communicating at close quarters with the village elder.* **Top:** *Those Urganaatha that remain on land live in deep caverns and caves. Despite the help of the Gestalt in overcoming their agorophobia, many older slugs remained petrified, and will emerge no further than these natural doorways from their caverns.* **Above:** *A Bierbeirb. Some reach 12 or 13 kilometres in diameter. Envoys to the Gestalt are selected from smaller specimens such as this female. The Bierbeirb maintain little or no contact with any other species but the Gestalt; they are at a stage of development approximately equivalent to our own Stone Age.* **Right:** *Gestalt travelling robot form. Before they decided to utilise the mindless bodies of the beautiful Simnimarians, the Gestalt used robot containers such as this to carry a fragment of their mind to worlds where physical presence was required.*

would be agreed and the boundaries drawn. Although the Ticireig accepted the invitation, their delegate committed ritual suicide at the start of the Conference, after declaring war on the Universe. The Ticireig remain in a state of war, against the Virmiri in particular. Their attacks on Human ships passing through the Night Wall in 7684 AE resulted in the Night Wars, which in a sense are continuing.

Although the Qa'Qal'Orq Gestalt wished to be present at the Conference, it did not wish to attend in a disembodied state and so sought a suitable host-body. The Virmiri suggested the inhabitants of Simnimar, a beautiful humanoid race whom they had discovered during their quest for Xanjust. The Simnimarians were devoid of any intellect, since a viral organism on the planet had once invaded their brains and rendered them incapable of thought. Although they behaved by instinct, thus continuing the race, the virus was transmitted during copulation, and the blankness perpetuated too. The Qa'Qal'Orq agreed to the Virmiri proposal and several members of the Gestalt entered the blank minds of the Simnimarians making them whole beings once more. Such was the Qa'Qal'Orq's pleasure at becoming creatures of the flesh again that after the conference, when they had no further use for physical forms, they did not abandon them completely. It became the habit of each member of the Gestalt to spend at least half its time in a Simnimarian body, experiencing physical pleasures. At the same time, they searched in the microscopic vastness of the brain for the killing virus, in the hope that one day they could return the Simnimarians to their rightful state. Despite the eons of time for which they had existed, the Qa'Qal'Orq had not forgotten their origins.

Strange life of the elf-Ratheyn

The creatures known as the Ratheyn live upon the planet Baralyon, which has a figure-of-eight orbit around the twin suns Yothanm (an orange giant) and Hodirf (a blue dwarf). Although both suns give equal heat to Baralyon, the overall intensity of radiation reaching the surface of the planet varies, depending on which sun is closest. This has caused the life forms of Baralyon to develop two distinct phases of existence. The Ratheyn in particular display a complete change in both their physical and mental characteristics as the planet moves from one sun to the other. When Yothanm is their primary, the Ratheyn are a placid, elf-like race with small, frail bodies. They inhabit hollow crystals, delicately carved into intricate shapes. They lead a calm, idyllic ex-

istence, feeding off the vegetable matter of the planet.

But as the Baralyon passes from Yothanm to Hodirf, the Ratheyn start their metamorphosis. First, they fall into a deep, coma-like trance. Then their limbs and torsos thicken. They secrete a substance from a gland in their necks which soon covers the entire body and hardens into a tough carapace. When Baralyon begins to orbit Hodirf, the Ratheyn emerge from their trances, completely transformed and with no memory of their previous existence. No longer are they gentle creatures, but bestial brutes who run amok over Baralyon, destroying the crystal cities and slaughtering the animal life of the world for food. By the time Baralyon has returned to orbit about Yothanm (20 Human years later), nothing remains of the Ratheyn's former homes, and they have to build them anew when they shed their carapaces and resume their lives in their elf-form.

This cycle (which occurs five times in the life of a Ratheyn) has continued remorselessly ever since the elf-Ratheyn evolved intelligence. Thanks to a Virmiri visitation in the sixth millennium, however, at least a small part of the world is now protected from the ravages of the beast-phase. The Virmiri observed the senseless destruction of the crystal houses and realized that if the Ratheyn were ever to truly progress as a race, then their continuous devolution into beasts must be thwarted. The Virmiri waited until Baralyon was orbiting Yothanm and the Ratheyn were in their elf-forms, then landed and told the Ratheyn what they had observed. The Ratheyn refused to believe them, but agreed that several of their number could visit Hiraldion where, the Virmiri promised, the Qa'Qal'Orq would convince them that they did, indeed, devolve into beasts whenever Baralyon orbited the sun Hodirf.

When the elf-Ratheyn arrived on Hiraldion, the Qa'Qal'Orq probed their minds and quickly discovered that it was the high level of P-rays from Hodirf which caused the Ratheyn to metamorphose. They uncovered and revealed, the Ratheyn's hidden ancestral memory of their beast form, thus forcing them to accept that they were the destroyers of their own creations. Until then, the elf-Ratheyn had explained the recurrent devastation to themselves by the myth of the Beasts of Night, who invaded the planet at the Times of Drifting (that is, when the Ratheyn were succumbing to the P-rays) and tore their ethereal home to pieces.

The elf-Ratheyn delegation returned to Baralyon and passed on this revelation to their tribe. From that time forward, whenever Baralyon began its approach to

Shillath, the conference world of the Qa'Qal'Orq and the meeting place for the intelligences of the Hiraldion Sector. This great and magnificent city was built by robots more than a million years ago. The city is intelligent and replenishes itself, melting and fashioning new structures out of the decaying remains of old. And yet it was still dying until the Gestalt made contact with it, and learned of the corrosion that was, year by year, reducing the availability of raw metal. Carefully directed asteroid-falls into the body of the city have now supplied the sentient organism with all the metal it requires; in return its deserted, and wealthy, spaces are made available for all manner of galactic conferences.

Edward Blair Wilkins

Previous page: A Valdorr, robot creature of the planet Ongaraaka. Legend often links the Valdorr robots with the fabulous city-world of Shillath. Were the Valdorr the builders who were given a world of their own after constructing Shillath? The robot Valdorr are benign, inventive, and content. They construct wonderful games and toys, such as these atmosphere skis. **Right:** *One form of the Valdorr tampered with its own structure, in an attempt to make itself more powerful; the result was the hostile race of robot beings known as the Belakk. They look peculiar, have difficulty with spare parts, and are the most aggressive robot form known.* **Above:** *Ongaraak itself, the world of the robots, covered with their structures, which are beautiful in a machine-oriented way.*

Hodirf, this small group of Ratheyn hid in the deep shafts of their crystal mines, protected from the sun's radiation, and remained in their elf-forms. Over the generations they have spread out, taking the word with them, and bringing more tribes into the sustained elf existence. Gradually the elf-Ratheyn have begun to progress further up the ladder of technological evolution.

The Firefalls of Olisco

Those few Human explorers and emissaries that have journeyed to this far distant Sector all, without exception, ask to see the Firefalls of Olisco. The reports they bring back are spoken in tones of wonder. The firefalls appear to be great flows of burning gas and organic liquid that cascade from plateaus over ten kilometres high. There are apparently over 400 such falls on the world, each completely covering the sheer walls of the plateau. The largest firefall, the circumference of the mountain, is 1000 kilometres long. The fire is caused by the organic

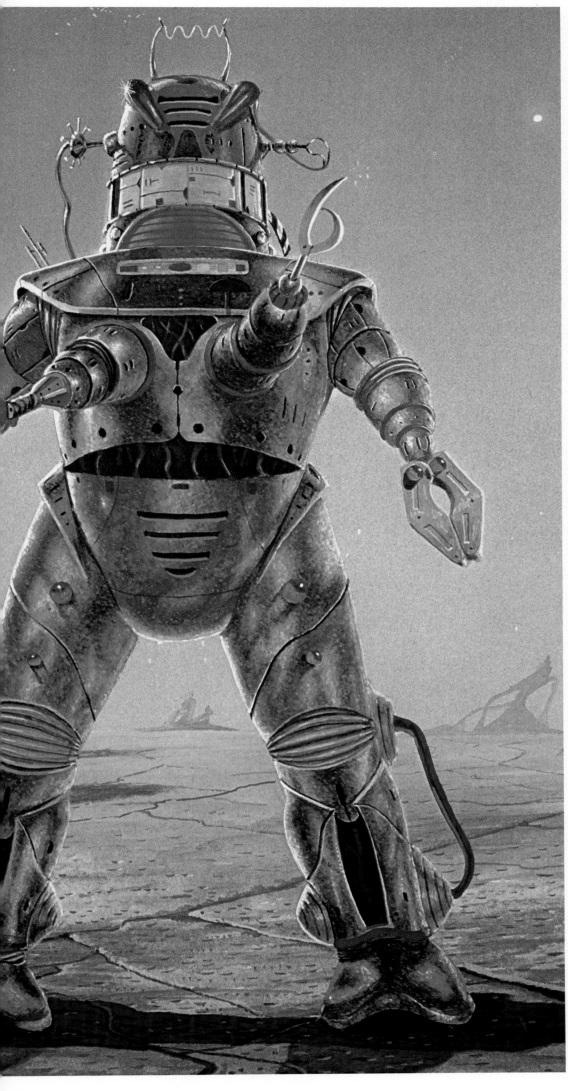

exudate from a plant form that flourishes on the high plateaus. The gas and liquid excreta are highly inflammable, and pour in channels from the deep jungles to the cliff edges, where they are ignited by the flames rising from below. The planet Olisco was for generations of the Qa'Qal'Orq thought to be uninhabited by any sentient life-form, but recently the Gestalt has reported that it has sensed minds living within the immense flames themselves. These creatures swim up and down the firefalls. They are fish-like and some 40 metres long. How they are protected from burning and upon what they feed, are questions that are, for the moment, unanswerable.

The Valdorr: robot creatures of Ongaraaka

One of the most unusual life forms discovered anywhere in the Universe is the machine life, or robot intelligence, known to the Qa'Qal'Orq as the Valdorr. Ongaraaka is close to the Night Wall limit of the Hiraldion Sector. It is a little known and little contacted world. Reports suggest that it is a ruin, covered with the industrial structures of a time when the crust was mined for practically anything, from organic fuels to decorative crystals such as diamonds and rubies. For this purpose, the now extinct inhabitants of Ongaraaka built self-replicating robots and implanted organic intelligence and awareness in them. Ongaraaka was not the only world where these creatures left robot equipment, and the immortal souls of a few of their kind. Some 40 worlds in the same galaxy are inhabited by similar machine intelligences.

How the Ongaraaki became extinct is not known, although a robot myth – the *Valldorr Cycle of Change*, an epic legend that takes a month to tell – hints strongly at mass poisoning by the waste products of their industrial obsession. Since the Ongaraaki themselves seem to have been reluctant to leave their homeworld, seeding no colonial worlds with anything but robots, the completeness of their extinction can be understood. Once they had gone, their robots continued and now form a viable, vital and genuinely evolving part of Alien Life.

In appearance they are not dissimilar to the sort of humanoid robot to which the Human Sector is accustomed. It is a sensible and stable form, even for creatures not themselves humanoid. They are benign and cooperative. It must also be remembered that they share a limited number of 'core minds', some 5000 original minds being replicated now many thousands of times over.

On the world Bersal, where the Ongaraaki seeded a few industrial robots, a regrettable evolution has occurred. Here the robots have tampered with their basic form and affected their programming. Known as the Belakk, this sub species is violent and unpredictable. They are evolving a space technology and could pose a considerable threat to the peace of the Sector within a millennia or two if not before.

4...NARATHNU SECTOR

DOMINANT INTELLIGENCE: NARATHNU/NARATHANA
INTELLIGENCE: HUMANOID ** INTELLIGENT LIFE FORMS:
188 BIOFORMED HUMANOID ** EARTH VERS OF
2088 NATIVE. # KNOWN OF GALAXIES: 8350 #KNOWN: OF KNOWN DOMINANCE: NATIVE NO.

Previous page: The Ivirom System, home solar system of the Narathnu. Ivirom is a bright yellow star, and no less than 40 planets orbit at distances ranging from 20 million miles to the cold depths of space, approximately where Jupiter is in our solar system. Nuxor, the homeworld of the Narathnu, is a small world in the centre of this chaos; it has eleven moons, and a sister planet called Nasara, shrouded in white cloud, and reminiscent of Venus. This was the first colonially inhabited world of the Narathnu, and the cause of the division of the species. Above: A symbolic mime of the invasion of Ayfaz by the Vargorn (performed by a Narathnu actor). Right: The Narathana are traders, and their trading ships are among the best in the known Universe. Big and well designed, they are able to transport whole zoo loads of animals in a variety of enclosed environments.

Native intelligent life in the Narathnu Sector evolved comparatively recently, although its rim galaxies had already been colonized by races from other Sectors. The Narathnu, whose homeworld Nuxor is one planet among 40 in the Ivirom System, are peaceable traders. Two races dominate their species. The tall, slender, copper-skinned Narathnu are accomplished dancers, musicians and storytellers. Their starships travel the settled worlds of their Sector staging elaborate pantomimes and musicals in exchange for the food and air supplies necessary for them to continue their long voyages through the galaxies of their zone.

The second race, known as the Narathana, are squat, olive-skinned, and looked down upon by the higher Narathnu. Their name, in fact, means 'lesser Narathnu'. They are traders in material goods, mostly metals, and will guarantee to supply anything, anytime, anywhere. This guarantee extends to providing specimens of other life forms for alien zoos. Unfortunately, the Narathana are so dominated by their trading instincts that they make no distinction between

intelligent and non-intelligent life. This has often been the cause of friction on those occasions when the Narathana have appropriated members of an intelligent race from their homeworld and delivered them to another world for study or exhibition. Human history abounds in examples of Narathanian kidnapping. Several races threatened war against the Narathnu (making no distinction between the two subspecies) and eventually the traders were forced to sign an agreement which prevents the transportation of intelligent life forms for the purpose of sale.

The Narathana are famed for knowing the location of every mineral resource, every drug and every exotic species of plant and animal in their Sector. Their trading monopoly has been the cause of much anger and controversy on worlds where it is felt that the Narathana charge exorbitant prices for their cargoes; but the Narathana point out that since they were the first race to explore the many worlds of their Sector, they are entitled to such a monopoly.

The only item which the Narathana are unable to freely obtain is the rare element

66

Left: Tales from the Dark Wheel enacted by Narathnu entertainers. These tell of heroes and heroines, of quests for hidden treasure, of invasion by the organised and brutal armies of despots, and the valiant resistance by small bands of forest living peoples, seeking their true king. All the tales have a familiar ring to them, and when the pictures that accompany the tales are studied carefully, it is quite clear that the Tales of the Dark Wheel are tales of Human beings.
Above: The Dark Wheel landings. The Human ship supposedly landed on a world peopled by small-winged reptilian forms, strikingly reminiscent of dragons, but this is myth adapting the features of the alien to suit the ancient legends of Earth. As can be seen, the inhabitants of the Dark Wheel have maintained a medieval appearance, carrying swords and building dark castles.

zotronium, found only in the giant comets of the Tirregon Federation, a cluster of galaxies in a remote area of the Sector. The peoples of the Tirregon Federation jealously guard their supplies of this radioactive element, which provides the fuel for the warp drives of the Narathnian starships. Since the Narathnu are constantly building new ships to take them on faster and longer voyages, they greatly depend on adequate supplies of zotronium. Thus the Tirregon Federation has been able to check Narathanian profiteering by threatening to withdraw their supplies of the element should the Narathana increase the prices of their goods too rapidly. It is a matter of some irony among the peoples of the Sector that their chief traders are themselves wholly dependent on other races for the raw material which they most require.

The Tale of the Dark Wheel

The copper-skinned Narathnu are noted mythmakers. One of their stories is the legend of the Great Ship, an account of a mysterious race that lives in the Dark Wheel – a galaxy named thus because it is shrouded in black clouds of intergalactic dust and gas. This race is indisputably Human, for they are bipedal, smooth-skinned, five-fingered, and have a legend of *uurth*, the Mother World that spawned them. Equally indisputable is the fact that they colonized the Dark Wheel while the Human race was still in the Stone Age.

It is now known that during the first phase of Humankind's expansion into the stars, a generation ship, populated by more than a million colonists, passed through a warp fault in space and was flung across time and space emerging into the Narathnu Sector at a time when no galaxies in that area had yet developed fully intelligent life. The Humans settled many worlds in the Dark Wheel, but it is thought that their passage through the warp hole had affected their minds, causing them to be intensely suspicious of contact with other intelligent races. The few Narathnu ships to enter the Dark Wheel were expelled after the briefest of exchanges with the Human worlds. Thus practically nothing is known of the nature of the Human civilization that has developed behind the dark clouds. Since rumours are rife that the Humans habitually exterminate any intelligent life to evolve in their galaxy, it is shunned and feared by most races elsewhere.

Multiple life forms in the Sector

The Narathnu Sector is noted for the variety of its life forms. Perhaps the strangest of these is the Graan, the Narathnian name for a binary system of stars which were thought to be unremarkable until observations of the sunspots on their surfaces indicated that they formed a regular pattern and seemed to take the form of a 'conversation' between the two stellar bodies. Further study of the stars has led to the belief that they are both intelligent. Does some form of sentient life, conditioned to high temperatures, exist within their seething, gaseous interiors like fish swimming in a sea, or do the stars themselves possess awareness? At present the precise nature of the Graan intelligence is still in doubt, since no race has succeeded in communicating with the stars. However, they continue to attract great interest and are regularly visited by a variety of races, many of whom see the Graan as the ultimate life form in the Universe, the state of being to which all species must eventually aspire.

Quite different from the Graan, but equally puzzling, are the Ulejj, of the tiny world of Caloum B. The Ulejj are tree-like plants. They breed by wind and insect pollination, obtain their food and water from the soil, practise photosynthesis, but are also capable of moving great distances during seasonal changes in temperature. They possess shallow roots which they are able to withdraw from the soil when the weather turns cold. Then they use these roots as 'legs' to carry them to warmer latitudes where they overwinter. The 'branches' of the trees are also mobile, and the Ulejj use them to embrace their fellow creatures, to pluck parasites from their trunks, and most importantly of all, to draw complex patterns in the soil. The meaning of these patterns has never been discovered, but many authorities argue that they are indicative of intelligent activity. There are also indications that the Ulejj possess an elaborate social hierarchy which is related to the number of blossoms which each plant produces and their exact colour and fragrance. Like the Graan, the Ulejj do not seem capable of communicating with other species, so their level of intelligence seems uncertain.

On the planet Ayfaz, a chill, windy world, there exists a species whose intelligence is undeniable but who nevertheless remain elusive. These are the Llemaru, a race of swift-moving, ethereal beings that can only ever be glimpsed out of the corner of the eye. The Llemaru, being bodiless, have built no artifacts nor made any visible impression on their home-planet: they live simply to ride the winds of Ayfaz. Their name derives from a Narathnian word meaning 'wind-sprite'. They are known to be sentient because visitors to their planet experience pleasant hallucinations which can be directly linked to the close presence of a Llemaru. Such hallucinations are generally held to be the Llemaru way of greeting newcomers to Ayfaz.

On Harmocohl, a large, high-gravity world, the most advanced life form is the Derlesh, a slug-like race whose lethargy and slowness of thought is legendary. Although they are a comparatively advanced species, the Derlesh have little ambition and even less energy. They spend most of their lives eating and basking in the sun. To the outside observer, the pace of their lives is intolerably slow. A group of Derlesh can be watched for several days without them exhibiting any

Edward Blair Wilkins

obvious activity. However, their apparent lethargy is related to the rate at which their brain functions: to a Derlesh, all other species move around at an incredible speed. Since the average life span of a Derlesh is one millennium, they have ample time to accomplish necessary tasks at their own slothful pace. The Narathnu tell a story of a Derlesh who never saw daylight, for each morning when he awoke he took so long to open his eyelids that the sun had set before he was able to gaze upon it.

Perhaps the most hated species in the Narathnu Sector is the Vargorn, who inhabit the world Grisnad. The Vargorn are also known as Mind Vampires. They are skeletal beings with blood-red eyes and translucent skins, fearsome to look at and extremely dangerous. These creatures, who can scarcely be called civilized even though they have developed a sophisticated technology, show an utter disregard for other life forms whose mentalities they invade telepathically and then destroy purely for sport.

The Vargorn evolved on a planet where the native life forms were extremely dangerous and it is believed that they developed their 'mind parasite' powers as a defence against the animals that threatened them. However, having extinguished all the rival life forms on Grisnad, the Vargorn then moved into space, attacking Narathnian tradeships and disrupting trade throughout the Sector. Soon they began to invade worlds, decimating entire populations with their ruthless mental powers. Eventually their progress was halted by the Jerodii Federation, a group of races who discovered that the Vargorn were attracted to their potential victims by the 'smell' of their fear. By employing anxiety-quelling drugs, the Federation was able to repulse the Vargorn, and eventually they were driven back to Grisnad. A permanent guard was then placed on their System. The Vargorn, victims of their own evolutionary processes, cannot resist their racial cravings and must therefore remain quarantined from all other races in the Sector.

*Previous page: Llemaru, wind sprite of the planet Ayfaz. The Llemaru are reputed to be impossible to see with the naked eye, but they can be seen by the camera eye, especially when they hover high above their world, practically in orbit. **Left:** A southern Delphoran. They are furry, ape-like, not particularly welcoming to intruders, and have no idea at all that their world is discus shaped, and that they are trapped at the southern extremity. **Above:** A saberay, or semi-sentient Guardian ship, patrolling the Vargorn System, and their planet Grisnad. The Vargorn are frightening creatures. International Law forbids the depiction of a Vargorn, who are imprisoned upon their own world. **Right:** A view of the Galaxy known as the Dark Wheel, the star city where a large human population has lived and evolved for a million years.*

Perhaps the strangest planet in the Sector is Delphore, which resembles Mesklin in the Human Sector. Delphore is a pill-, or discus-shaped world, which spins about its short axis. Due to the planet's odd shape, its surface gravity decreases sharply as the flattened equator is reached. Two intelligent species have evolved independently at its north and south poles, adapted to the phenomenally high gravity. Low gravity is intolerable to each species. Consequently, neither race has ever left its polar region, and they remain unaware of each other's existence. The northern Delphorians, whose civilization is still primitive, believe that they live on the top of a great mountain, and must remain there; if they venture down its slope the gods will drag them into hell. The southern Delphorians, who are somewhat more advanced, have discovered the shape of their world and they mistakenly believe that all other heavenly bodies must be like it.

The Delphorians have not yet developed space travel and are unaware of intelligent life elsewhere. The spacefaring races of the Narathnu Sector are therefore forbidden to visit their planet in accordance with the Law of NonInterference, which states that all intelligent species evolving towards a technological society must be allowed to progress at their own pace with no outside interference.

Of all the races of creatures in the Narathnu Sector, none has succeeded in adapting to its environment more successfully than the polymorphs of the world Svanne, who are known to the Narathnu as the Salag. The Salag possess the remarkable ability to change the shape and structure of their bodies. In the early days of their development, Svanne's orbit was highly unstable and hence its climate was prone to abrupt changes. The Salag polymorphs evolved a flexible genetic code which enabled them to adapt their bodies to the prevailing climatic conditions. Over several millennia this evolutionary inheritance was developed and refined so that eventually the polymorphs could mimic the exact shape of any animal life form on their planet. Because they were intelligent, they had a natural advantage over the beasts which they were mimicking. So the original species of animal soon died out. Although today there still exists a great variety of animal forms on Svanne, every one of them is a Salag polymorph. Ironically, the original shape of the polymorphs is now unknown.

The most recent intelligent species to emerge in the Narathnu Sector is Wezeril, of the planet Quarak. Quarak is a gas giant similar to Jupiter, and the Wezeril evolved as jellyfish-like creatures who swam in its turbulent methane and hydrogen atmosphere. They developed no technology, but learned to travel in space by cocooning themselves in a vast envelope of Quarak's atmosphere, held to them by

powerful, mentally-generated electro-static forces, and then floating off into space like miniature planets, propelled by the solar wind. At such slow speeds, it would have taken them eons to reach other star systems had not Narathnu tradeships encountered them. The Narathnu detected the telepathic emanations which indicated intelligent beings and contact was quickly established. The traders, discovering the Wezeril's purpose, quickly struck up a bargain. The Narathana were methane breathers, and the Wezeril agreed to supplement their tradeship's atmospheres from the cocoons of methane which they carried about them. In exchange, the Narathana would transport Wezeril travellers to other star systems in their own ships. Thus the Wezeril were provided with the means to reach worlds far more quickly than before, while the Narathana had once again demonstrated the unique enterprise and bargaining capabilities which have brought them to preeminence in the Sector which bears their name.

Nuxor: World of Steel

The home world of the Narathnu traders can no longer be seen, although some complain it can be seen too clearly. Reminiscent of the now legendary Trantor of the Human Sector, the tiny world of Nuxor, one of 40 worlds in the Narathnu sun system, soon became designated as the Central Coordination World for the expanding and gigantic Narathnu trade operation. With few oceans on the world, despite an enormous underground reservoir of free water, the planet Nuxor was ideal for the purposes of conversion into a single city. At first there were 20 cities, built on the ruins of ancient and primitive sites, still precious to the Narathnu. These are now protected beneath the new metal skin, which was built on stilts so that the ground and relics below might be preserved for all time (Earth and Trantor systematically destroyed every trace of their prespace history).

As the Narathnu Empire expanded, so the cities expanded: one city controlled the documentation of populations on the Federation of Worlds that fell under Narathnu control; another was set up to store the facts of available resources upon those worlds; another administered the Narathnu sun system itself, and so on. As the cities expanded, so at last they touched, and fused, and even began to spread across each other. Heat built up in this enormous system, so reflector and radiator panels were built around the whole world, shining brilliant purple to the observer on any approaching ship. Nuxor is as bright as Ivirom itself. Not surprisingly it is a major tourist attraction.

Around the quintet of planets associated with Nuxor – Ixor, Traxor, Megarra,

Minoxil and Ferrix – is gathered the space fleet. Over a million vessels are supposed to be moored by space anchor at any one time in the vicinity of the six worlds. It is said that the gravitational field in the area changes so frequently that Nuxor never orbits its sun in the same way twice. Certainly, the attraction between the six worlds is frighteningly large, and the cause of many earthquakes, floods and cracks in the steel skin of Nuxor itself. The densely packed asteroidal belts, the remnants of even more clustered fields of space debris now substantially cleared by fission bomb, suggest that in the past several other closely associated worlds have broken up underneath the gravitational stress.

The Legend of the Star Lake

This legend was recorded from a Narathnian storyteller during a trade meeting between crystal traders of the Seven Suns Galaxy – part of the Narathnu Sector – and Human observers on Jhauvian Station. This Narathnu, a copper skin he was, and a lone trader in those early days when Nuxor was yet earth and stone, and the Night Wall, it is told, burned brilliant ochre across the Universe, not dark and deadly as it is today. In a small ship, lost against the brilliance of the stars, this Narathnu of name Nophenmep, auk r'Leki, which means Nophenmep of the third cell line of Leki, came upon a lake of stars, that spread before him and was depthless and beautiful and sucked him in. His tiny ship was swept about the lake, from star to star, riding the ripples of light and gravity as if he was in a small boat travelling about the whirlpool that will finally suck the luckless down. Here was a place, then, where the stars had melted together, to form a lake of crystal fire, a liquid lake with creatures that swam in its depths, beyond space and time and reason. Some there were that poked their eyes above the pool of fire, and peered across the miles at the struggling trader, waiting for his fragile ship to be drawn below the lake.

In time this Narathnu, Nophenmep, resigned himself to death, and ceased to struggle. Twice about the lake of stars he had travelled, and knew this pool of fire to span a void wider than the void between galaxies: an immense lake of stars. Down he sank, down into the coloured fire storms below, through the levels of space and time, at once in past and future, on this end and that end of the Universe, oscillating between places as far distant as thought can comprehend. Giant creatures swam there, their bodies dripping tongues of purple flame, their brains the pulsing, spinning forms of the dark compacted stars when death has taken all their light. Here the illusion, and delusion, broke: clear of mind and of eye he found

A Wezeril, giant jelloid creature from the planet Quarak. The Wezeril are of low intelligence. They are self-aware and have a concept of an afterlife, but they have not developed the basic concepts of mathematics, and a physical understanding of the structure of matter. The Wezeril begin life as tiny disc-shaped larvae, swimming in shoals of several millions in the seas of Quarak. As the years pass, certain larvae are selected for growth, and eventually, from every group, just two emerge, ingesting the mass of the others and growing to the enormous adult size.

Top: Nuxor, the great home-world of the Narathnu, has been transformed by the amazing love of technology, and building, into a single-city world, the solid metallic shell being broken only by the sprawling parks and outdoor entertainment stages. **Above:** *Inside Nuxor, with so much of its land surface hidden by the city, there are problems with heat disposal. Deep in the planetary crust power houses, such as this, tap the very magma for heat.* **Right:** *Polymorphs of Svanne. One of the most unusual of any of the life forms in the Universe are the salag as they are known to the Narathnu. They are amorphous creatures with shape changing ability.*

himself to be travelling through a tunnel of swirling light, towards a place that he could see was a spread of bright and wonderful stars, all reds and golds and youthful firecolours, a young galaxy, newly coalesced, and bursting with life. The journey through this tube of space seemed to take forever. He experienced fear, then sadness, then wonder, then anger. In time, and perhaps after a tenth of his life had past, he emerged into dark space, floating between the stars, close to a sun where he could detect a hundred worlds. Behind him he could see an almost invisible spinning disc, a wide pool of darkness that turned away from him as he

watched, here flickering redly, and yellowly, a glancing of light that showed its spinning form. He journeyed among the worlds and found them all dead, all ruined. Everywhere were the metal cities of a great race, everywhere the space yards of a travelling race, everywhere the parks and cities, the roadways and temples of a people who knew both religion and science, and loved them both. It was they who had built the gateway through the stars, the spinning lakes of light and dark that, between them, covered ten times the distance of our Universal Sector.

Where was this world? Nowhere in Known Space; nowhere where Humans

Above: Smurlik, worm-creatures of the planet Simura IV. The Smurlik are immense, able to swallow whole machines, and to project energy. *Right:* Derlesh, slug creatures from Hamarcohl. The Derlesh are justly famed for their amazing lethargy. Communication is difficult, as it takes weeks for the slugs to nod their heads in answer to a question. The Narathnu have devised chemical communication capsules, one of which is being shot into a chieftain's mouth in this picture. The chemical will enter the Derlesh's blood stream, and elicit a faster response (about 10 days) to the encoded question. *Far right:* The Ulejj, strange tree-form creatures of the planet Caburn B. The intelligent plants drift about the planet on 'organic islands', which behave like clouds, sucking up moisture from the surface below.

have walked, or Oisir-Raxxla, nowhere where those mind beings of the distant places have ever probed. The lake of stars spins onwards through the Night Wall.

Night Wraiths of Fierforag

During the war between the Narathnu and the worm-like creatures known as the Smurlik, intelligences from the world of Simura IV who fought the Narathnu on a principle of honour, a strange force of destruction was manifest on the planetside field of battle. Narathnu military troops, an elite corps of infantrymen, were decimated by wraiths, tall smokey apparitions that whirled about the field of combat, untouchable, invincible, deadly. The flash of light that accompanied their strike was thought to be from a light sword, the

wounds inflicted are like those of such primitive weapons.

Much later, the Narathnu made an uneasy peace with the Smurlik and learned of the world of Fierforag, and its high life form, which the Smurlik called Night Wraiths. The Wraiths were creatures that had evolved from winged ancestors who had become extremely light, and extremely fast, supplementing their speed through the air by the use of teleportation. Ultimately the teleport ability was lost, as were the wings. On the ground, confined to surface niches, the Wraiths grew in size, but retained the ability to move instantly and rapidly across short distances. Thus they appear to flicker in and out of vision and, of course, are practically unopposable in battle.

DOMINANT INTELLIGENCE: VAN-IREC... MULTI-
FORMED, EXOSKELETAL.... INTELLIGENT LIFE
OF SAME: INTELLIGENT *# EARTH YEARS
DOMINANCE: 11880 3900 EXTANT
OF DOMINANCE: #8 NO. OF GALAXIES: 1257

Graham Wildridge

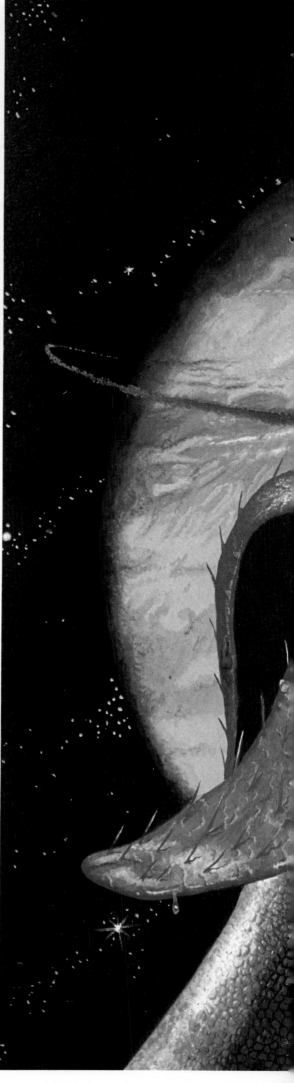

*Previous page: Madrigallax, the homeworld of the Uan-irec. Once a richly forested world, basking beneath a brilliant yellow sun, Madrigallax is now a world typical of the effects of a long, sustained assault upon it by a war-orientated intelligent race. Madrigallax is now a museum, a remnant of its former majesty, and supports scarcely two million of the creatures it spawned. Their crystalline structures rise majestically, and brilliantly, into the dusk-scape, attracting tourists; objects of wonder, no Uan-irec can explain the meaning behind them, so far have they distanced themselves from their origins. Some Uan-irec still live there, clustering at the equator in vast, steel-shelled castles reminiscent of the mud and stone forts of their early days. **Above:** Of the original Uan-irec form very little evidence remains, although their paintings, many of which are stored in such crystal structures as scatter their world today, suggest that before they evolved into their hundreds of castes, they were very much like bees. **Right:** Did the Uan-irec visit Earth in the very early days of their conquest of space? This nectar-drinking caste, which will be eaten by the soldier castes when it is full, is seen taking the organic molecules from a plant unknown to Earth, but the planet in the background is strongly reminiscent of Jupiter which is situated in the same solar system.*

In this rich, but small, Universal Sector, abundant in the remains of previous dominating species, the insect-like Uan-irec are only the latest in a long succession of Galactic Rulers. The Sector lies close to that area of space ruled by Humans, separated from it by the sparsely populated Null Zone of Garamond's Rift. Evidence of free travel between the two is abundant, both by those races that predated Humankind in their own Sector and by the various species that have existed in the Uan-irec Zone and have discovered the secret of warp space, thus gaining the ability to travel by thruspace.

The Uan-irec are warriors, and their social structure is based on castes, some 150 of them. More than 80 castes indicate warrior status. Strangely, the Uan-irec are not avaricious, are not given to conquest, and do not seek the destruction and subjugation of other worlds in the fashion, say, of the Oisir-Raxxla. Nonetheless, they are obsessed by war, honour, and the testing of strength. They regard war not just as an art form, but as a sacred expression of their place in the Universe. They cannot comprehend that the destruction of non-Uan-irec intelligence might in some way add to their understanding of the nature of war, and so they do not actively seek

hostilities outside of their own race. Nevertheless, they have been involved in some very bitter, and very bloody, wars in space, one of which, the so-called Insect War, was with the Iltronian colonies of the Human race. To the Uan-irec it is unforgivable that any race should deny them the knowledge they seek; they have the irksome habit of descending upon a planet and assuming they may take what they require without asking. They respond to any objection according to their whim – perhaps by mounting a full-scale planetary invasion, perhaps with nothing more than a Duel of Champions.

The Uan-irec are peculiar in that, despite their sophisticated space technology, they fight and make war with traditional and ancient weapons, regarding several such as sacred. Their whole social and economic structure is set around the learning of new weaponry; they are willing to learn techniques, styles and usages from any and all of the great cultures of their own and any other Universal Sectors. They have journeyed as far as they possibly can seeking out weapons against which they cannot stand, learning about them, and learning to oppose them. Their means of payment for such education and experience is to fight

as mercenaries for those cultures that have instructed them in any war of their own.

The evolution of the Uan-irec towards this strange destiny is one of the better documented developments from other Sectors. They arose, more than four million years ago, on the windy, forested world of Madrigallix, evolving from solitary creatures, who tapped the sap of certain trees. into communal creatures gathered in central castles. It was not long, in evolutionary time, before they began to develop a sophisticated and complex social caste structure. Although they were still unintelligent, their 'castles', made of compacted soil and rock, soon rose high above the forests, their surfaces brilliant silver with the excretion from the bodies of the worker castes. A single city could cover an area of 500 hectares, and plunge below the earth to the breeding warrens to a depth of 2000 metres. Their greatest threat came from the flying life forms of Madrigallax, some of which were possessed of rudimentary awareness, and which fed upon the young, unarmoured Uan-irec.

Over the millennia the dangers grew in number until eventually the survival of the Uan-irec was constantly contested. Their castles had grown so high that there was a simultaneous danger of the structures collapsing – and indeed many did, exterminating the resident colonies. Across the planet, however, certain castes of Uan-irec evolved who possessed the intuitive comprehension of the use of environment – stone, wood, metal rods from the lava fields – and they strengthened their castles into 'holds' in the classical sense, making them harder to destroy. From this caste came the power of intelligence and self awareness, and the Uan-irec rapidly grew into a technological culture.

It is a Universal law that a race is motivated by the collective unconscious, which draws much of its direction from events in early history. Remembered half as myth, half as contemporary social mores, the power of the past is always stronger than suspected. The Uan-irec, although they had long forgotten the events in question, were driven into their state of warrior obsession by early help given them by a visiting colony ship from – it seems most likely – the Oisir-Raxxla Sector. Facing an almost overwhelming threat from the sky-living Ptermaridi, vast, winged creatures with an advanced tool-using ability, and a pleasant habit of dropping pointed stakes and fire boulders upon the Uan-irec castles, the Uan-irec transmitted their distress on the subspace waves that carry emotions. Fifty ships from a strange race, bearing fire weapons and the technology to construct arrows that could be launched from gigantic vine and wood bows, descended upon the world and saved the Uan-irec from destruction. From then on the Uan-irec became obsessed with learning weapon techniques from all across the void, and their space technology grew out of this desire. The stories of the weapons owned by star-living races were the elixir of life

David Hardy

*Left: Uan-irec skirmishing on the world Jholath, against unknown creatures. The Uan-irec are adaptable warriors. Here an Uan-irec soldier is dressed identically and carrying the same weapons as the invading forces with whom the Uan-irec were acting as mercenaries. **Above:** The Uan-irec literally gutted the other worlds of their system for the raw materials for weapons, spaceships and floating cities. In this picture of their krondinium excavations on an asteroid their sun, Madrigal B can be seen in the background, with a tiny black hole close to it; this sucks matter and energy from the sun, which is one reason why Madrigal B has aged so fast. The soldier caste evolved early in the life of the Uan-irec. and its adaptability is a function of the racist desire to fight on all worlds and with all the forms of life it can find. These warriors are of the holy caste of the flame bearers, soldiers trained to perfection in laser and phaser weapons, and able to draw upon their own body energy to maintain power in their hand guns. The caste would be unable to perform in conditions demanding hand-to-hand combat and would most likely undergo a form of suicide. From the organic remains, however, a new warrior would arise, from asexual reproduction. This drone would be a mindless functionary adapted in the crudest possible way to the new planetary conditions.*

*Above: When man fought the Ezraaq for possession of the so-called Jhauvian Void, the Uan-irec sent mercenaries to help. A typical battle scene is shown here, with one Human surrounded by the small, lobster-like caste known as Dread Jaws. Soldier castes are represented as well. **Right:** Uan-irec castles. Tall, majestic and beautiful, they are built of metal alloys that do not corrode. Inside each castle live a million beings; the castles, as in times gone by, plunge down into the earth, a great honeycomb of passages and chambers, metal lined and secure. The accumulated knowledge of the Uan-irec is stored here with the sacred collections of weapons, the portraits of their great heroes, and written accounts of their great battles, and quests for the learning of new weapons.*

to them; the sense of honour, of help, was driven into their genetic codes by the simple selection for altruism. Memory of the Oisir-Raxxla remained as 'those from the Sword of the Stars', and the quest for the Sword of the Stars became the basic drive of the Uan-irec: the search for that weapon of legend which, once wielded by a warrior of unsullied honour, would render him as one with the Weapons Lord, and give him total control over all weapons in the Universe.

Although the Uan-irec society was already diversified into many castes, a proliferation of warrior castes now arose, mostly by natural selection. Twenty of

them were brought about by genetic engineering: these castes were called the Holy Castes of the Sword. The Living Shield was a caste who possessed no weapons but whose bodies could twist and deform into shield walls, with half-metre thick chitinous surfaces that could absorb a considerable explosive power; the Living Bomb, similarly, carried natural gases within its body and could ignite them by a bio-electric spark, destroying a wide area; the Weapons Master was one trained in each and every weapon encountered by the Uan-irec, the bearer of the sacred knowledge of death, destined to demonstrate the use of the weapon and transmit the Power of Life into the first Uan-irec equivalent by being sacrificed to that newly forged or fashioned tool of destruction; the Dart Thrower and the Chitin Arrow could produce these weapons in special glands in their immense bodies, and use mechanical power to fling them hundreds of metres; the Harpie caste had learned to fly, and in the fashion of their ancient enemy the Ptermaridi could launch arrows and stones from the sky; the Mech had evolved limbs on which weapons could be tied or fitted: the huge, slashing claws of the Axe caste could be cut from the dead Axe and fitted onto the body of a Mech. At the top of the caste list was the Flame Lord, the most sacred of the social orders, almost priest-like in his power: he could breathe fire and was the traditional carrier of the Fire Sword, an ancient relic reputedly left by the warriors who had helped the Uan-irec in those long ago times, warrior subjects of the Sword of the Stars.

In the course of their exploration of the Universe, the Uan-irec made contact with practically every intelligent alien species in their Sector, most of which still exist in the tenth millennium. From each race the Uan-irec learned weapons techniques both bizarre, and occasionally practical.

On the world Shulmeirik they encountered the ghostly Cirag, spirit creatures nearly 2000 metres tall, which flow like immense jellyfish; not surprisingly they have become known, in Human jargon, as the Ghosts of Shulmeirik. Intelligent creatures, the Cirag have no technology as such. They exist half in our reality, and half in an alternative reality. Legend has it that each creature contains spirits of the dead of other worlds, but this is manifest nonsense. The Cirag are certainly aware of the existence of other races, and taught the Uan-irec the so-called 'spell of fading', by which, using mental energy in combination with the exudate of a symbiotic creature that lives abundantly on Shulmeirik, and which are carried within the body spaces of the Cirag, the body may be made less physical, to the confusion of the enemy.

Close to the silent space that borders their Sector, the Uan-irec discovered the world Yovath, with its race of tiny creatures the Yovarii; very Human in many respects, except that they are only fist-sized, the Yovarii have known the secret of warp space for generations, and trade with the surrounding space on a vast scale. They have colonized a number of worlds, but their tiny stature has caused many problems; the average Universal height or size is 50 metres, whereas the tallest known Yovarii stood 25 centimetres high and was a giant among his people. Despite the size difference, the Yovarii instructed the Uan-irec in the use of the *akora*, a weapon not unlike the Human *bolas*, which they used to bring down not just enemies, but the spindly-legged spiders upon which they fed.

The Uan-irec almost certainly discovered the Ologog, of the ocean-covered world of Gabragorn II, in the same manner as early Human explorers discovered them, by following mysterious subspace signals to a source world that seemed, at first, deserted. The signals were distress signals, and Human biologists noted the similarity between them and the distress signals of dolphins that have been transported to other worlds and become lost in the unfamiliar deeps. Exploration teams were dispatched immediately, travelling carefully, for at this time the Humans were at war with the Uan-irec over the latter's destruction of a colonized world in the Human Sector. The first expedition to descend to the watery surface waited several weeks for contact with the creatures that were sending out the distress signals. In the words of the commander of that expeditionary force:

Inevitably the suggestion was made that the ocean itself was sentient, in the manner of Solaris in our own Sector. And yet, all analysis of this ocean showed it to be no more than water, saline, and a dilute mixture of organic molecules of not much complexity. We waited out the weeks, noting that the signals had changed, and seemed to be coming from a much closer source than at first. Eventually our sensors registered the approach of five creatures, from the trenches of the ocean that we estimate to be 80 kilometres deep. The submarine vessels that eventually surfaced shocked us to the core; we had seen the darkening of the waters for some days, and rapidly realized that the creatures were approaching in machines. The turbulence that accompanied the surfacing was almost fatal, but at last we floated there, in the dusk of the red sun, surrounded by six vessels that towered hundreds of metres above us. We waited for the creatures to appear, meanwhile communicating with them. We learned they were called the Ologog, and they were seeking a way to return to the mobile forms of their ancestors. It was at this time that we began to realize it was the ocean vessels themselves that were the intelligent creatures.

Thousands of years before, when the oceans had risen to cover the land, the Ologog, spindly, insectoidal creatures, had constructed immense sea cities, and placed in each the awareness of their kings. In the course of time, however, the biological life forms had become extinct. Their cities remained, however, to drift the deep oceans, their intelligence trap-

Above: *The ologog. Human contact with the ologog of Gabragorn II has been nearly as extensive as that by Uan-irec; the warrior castes have little interest in intelligences that cannot instruct them in new ways of war, but the ologog are sad and troubled creatures, and mankind has attempted to alleviate their burden. Communication with the ologog is made using large message capsules, which sink to the immense machine-creatures as they bask on the sea-bed.* **Right:** *Ghosts of Shulmeirik. Existing half in one reality, and half in another, the ghostly cirag, as they are correctly known, are untroublesome, intelligent creatures that nonetheless can give fellow creatures a nasty fright. They are often vast, up to 2000 metres tall, and they flow about their world, undulating gently, always inquisitive. Communication with them is slight. They have no technology, but clearly are fascinated by machines, flowing into their inner spaces and causing difficulties for such exploration teams as are shown here.*

ped in the wires and circuits of the submarine brains – submarine behemoths, immortal, pointless.

The Uan-irec learned nothing from the Ologog, and like the Humans were unable to help. They learned no weapons technique, either, from the strangest and most incomprehensible race ever encountered: the Blue, a name derived from their colour, which is practically all that could be discerned of the energy spirals and drifting forms of this bizarre race. They occupy Ciraq, a world infested with truly ancient ruins, too decayed to properly excavate and analyze. No doubt in the dim and distant past, the Blue had physical form as well as mental, but now they are beings of pure energy, and totally alien to Human and Uan-irec alike.

If there was no empathy between Blue and Uan-irec, the same cannot be said of the Knights of Zircix. Where they came from, this muscular, humanoid warrior elite, is not known; some have suggested Earth, but the internal anatomy of the creatures is not human, and they have a

small caste system of their own, which involves different physical forms. The Uan-irec discovered the Zircix Knights by chance. They happened upon a modest solar war in their Sector, participated, and observed the presence of mysterious mercenary forces. Following the mercenaries back to their homeworld, the Uan-irec discovered the Knights of Zircix, on the barren, rocky world of Zircierix.

Although the elite Knights lived here, they were not of this place originally. They had built castles and underground holds. The world was covered by their airways and arenas. Every day on the world a thousand duels were occurring, for the sake of practice, ready for the next call for help. The Knights do not breed, but are alleged to be grown in organ banks from the brain cells of the Great Lord of Arms, the first Knight, whose corpse lies in suspended animation hidden at the core of the dead world.

The Knights instructed the Uan-irec in the use of light sword, energy bolt, vibration axe, *direk* knife and the martial art

86

Eddie Jones

of *shiriwayak*, in which the internal organs are everted through the mouth and used in a deadly fashion. And it was the Knights who told of the distant world where a hundred different cultures used a thousand different weapons, certainly primitive, but of immense effectiveness. Thus, 12000 years ago, the Uan-irec came to Earth.

Their legends are filled with heroic tales of their adventuring among men, fighting as mercenaries against the Goths, the Mongols, Indian tribes, the Goths again, against the Saxons, *for* the Saxons, and for the cannibal tribes of polynesia. They assisted Caesar in his conquest of Europe, an achievement that has always seemed unlikely even for a man such as that great general. They had learned the art of siege, and the use of bodies of men as a weapon. They assisted the High King of Ireland, Brion mac Aenghus, in his war against the Britons, in exchange for instruction on how to use the deadly, near legendary *gae bolga*, the most hideous spear known to the races of Earth. They learned the art of the *boomerang*, and in exchange drew a map of the southern oceans for those tribes that wished to journey afar among the profusions of islands. They learned the art of the bow and stone-headed arrow from the Plains Indians of America and set up a field of force about the enormous continent to prevent the tribes from being interfered with for all of time. Unfortunately, the field decayed, although part of it remains intact, off the coastline of Florida.

An uneasy, but most likely permanent, peace exists today between the Humans and the Uan-irec. Earth no longer has weapons that are of interest to that war-hungry race. Instead, exploration permission has been granted to select bands of the warrior elite to scour the Human Sector for a world, and a life form, that can instruct them thoroughly in the use and application of that most primitive of weapons: the club.

Strange rituals of the Grillka'shanaskilk

The Grill, as they are more conveniently known, are indigenous to the water world Magog IV. Reptilian to look at, because of their green colouring and dry scales, the Grill are in fact warm-blooded, intelligent, viviparous and more closely analogous with mammals. They have a high level of technology, such as central heating for their undersea communal houses, and an efficient waste disposal system. They have never achieved space flight, although their existence is known to many of the space travelling races in their vicinity of the Universe. The Grill themselves are

familiar with the traders, and with the Uan-irec who overLord their world.

An otherwise sedate, almost dull race, they are most famous for their complex rituals, such as the death and water ritual. An aging queen lays a last batch of eggs into the water, instead of retaining the hatchlings in her body. As she absorbs water into her tissues she swells into an enormous balloon; when the eggs hatch the young Grill burrow into this sac of liquid and await the rotting of the carcase. They then emerge and the females contest the role of 'queen', fighting each other viciously until only four are left; these four then select mates, eat the remaining Grill, and descend into the deep oceans for a ritual that has, as yet, been undocumented, but which is referred to in the records as *in oceanis copularis franticaris*.

The Zoni Federation

On the border of Uan-irec space and the Null Zone of Garamond's Rift lies the small system of stars known as the Zoni Federation. The Zoni are aggressive, naive warriors, with a primitive space technology, and an avaricious jealousy for all wealth produced in those few worlds they overLord. The Uan-irec have left them well alone, after learning the use of the frightening 'fear stick', the energy-beam rifle that can interfere with the emotional state of the enemy. However dirithium resources in non-inhabited planets of the Zoni system and an immense reserve of natural oil, led to attempts by both the Human Federation, and a small consortium of worlds from the Null Zone known as the Thangan Empire, to contest the overLordship of these several Zoni planets. The central Zoni world of Jaimbaliz became the scene of a three-way land war. The invading forces were routed by the elite Zoni rifle riders. Their chitinous skin and body thorns, were a frightening sight to the Thangan amphiboids, whose darkest dreams were filled with memories of their ancient predators, creatures not unlike the red-eyed Zoni in appearance. In later years the Zoni warriors became something of a hero class, their technology being played down and their achievement in defeating a relatively small and badly equipped force of aliens correspondingly inflated to epic proportions.

Guardians of Lioness

At the edge of the Uan-irec Sector, the tiny, lush world of Lioness orbits its brilliant primary, the sole daughter of the sun, and a world as attractive to Humans as it is to the overLords themselves. Here live the results of an ancient genetic engineering

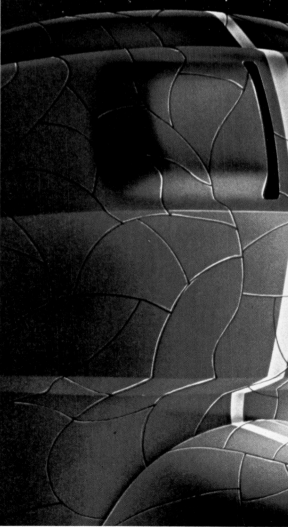

Above right: The strangest race ever encountered by the Uan-irec are the Blue, energy beings that confused and confounded the senses. This holograph of a Uan-irec ship skimming the surface of the Blues' world, Ciraq, shows the physical manifestation of a creative identifiable as an Uan-irec Living Shield . . . it is, in fact, the only form of communication ever attempted by Blues, the formation of replicas of visiting species. It can be alarming and is ultimately non-productive.
Right: Yovarii, tiny simian creatures of Yovath. The Yovarii are tiny even by Human standards, the tallest being no bigger than a man's clenched fist. This makes contact difficult, and the Uan-irec have developed tiny, fist-sized robots to do the job for them. The simioids have no idea that the robots are not the intelligent species they have heard so much about. The Yovarii have few weapons and a very primitive space technology.

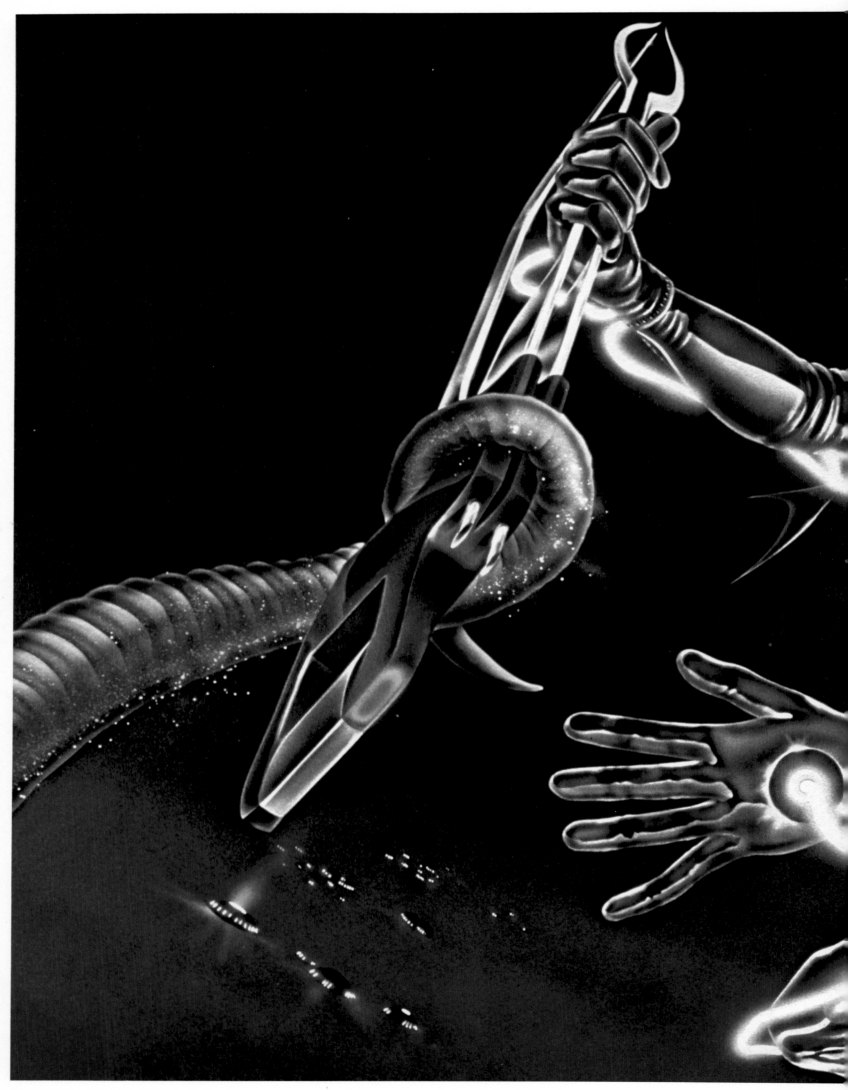

Previous page: Making contact with a Grillka'-shanaskilk, one of the giant, reptilian creatures of Magog IV. The Grill have a number of bizarre rituals that seem quite cruel and destructive to man and Uan-irec both. Both races are attempting to understand the reptilians better, and this particular underwater contact is a common sight on Magog. **Above left:** *The Uan-irec erect vast statues to their various teachers, and it seems apparent that the great Hector, famous from the Greek Wars with Troy, is one of them.* **Above right:** *Guardians of Lioness, a planet populated by chameleon and hybrid creatures, such as this half man, half cat being. The world is constantly visited by various races who seek out evidence that their own worlds had been tampered with by the race known as the Maath mithragi.* **Right:** *Giant rock lizard, crossed with a Virmiri, this fertile species of animal, found on Lioness and evidently the work of a genetic engineering programme, has lost its intelligence.*

experiment, undertaken by the then dominant race, the Maath'mithragi. Tall beings, elf-like in appearance, they were capable of levitation and movement on the astral plane, to which infraUniverse they ultimately declined.

At a time when the Uan-irac were scuttling creatures, building dirt castles in the sky, the Maath'mithragi surveyed the galaxies and interworlds as far as the Night Wall itself; they knew all, they loved all, and they cared for all. They were, themselves, a race that abhorred violence, so much so that each time they met a hostile, all-conquering planetary race they would resort to emotion and bribery to quell the dark hearts; but from beyond the Night Wall had come a race determined to subdue all worlds in their path; from the description, it seems certain they were the Oisir-Raxxla. The Maath'mithragi, disconsolate, defeated, dying, dedicated themselves to the task of saving those poor beings they had to insensitively created from the seeds of so much life. The world of Lioness was selected, and here a motley group of fertile chameleons was left. They have evolved into the Guardians of today.

Music World: Wyath.

One of the strangest worlds in the Uan-irec Sector is the planet Wyath, fourth world of the binary star Algon. The planet has

never known the natural development of intelligent animal life; in fact its natural fauna was very limited, although it boasted several magnificent forests and whole continents of brightly coloured flowers. Obsessed by the world's beauty, and aware of the natural system of caverns and passageways that honeycombed the planet's skin – some rising into sheer columns and cliffs that had been upthrust by crustal movements – the Uan-irec engineered the whole world into a single musical instrument. This love of natural sound is a fact often overlooked by students of the Uan-irec, who cannot equate the search for weapons with a love of art.

Each continent of Wyath produces a different medley of sounds. Each pinnacle, with its scattered caves, has been artfully altered to make it produce a sound of a different tone. The underground passages that emerge through 'blow holes' at regular intervals can produce sustained, changing melodies depending on the width of the 'control' gap, a single cave, half blocked by a movable rock, and under the guidance of the conductor.

It is to Wyath that the Uan-irec come to celebrate their achievements on the field of battle. It is here that they bring emissaries of other worlds; and it is to Wyath that they come to die, surrounded by the music of the earth that will take their

Above right: Zoni Warrior, with his body thorns trimmed away to make him a more efficient fighting machine. The Uan-irec learned much from these violent and cruel warriors, especially the use of the shameer, the great, wide bladed sword that could glide through a body in an instant without the slain warrior realising until the very moment his body fell to pieces. The shield the Zoni carries shows of an Uan-irec soldier caste, a terrifying mask indeed, and a sign of the mutual respect that both Zoni and Uan-irec held for each other. *Above left: An Uan-irec soldier caste,* his limbs adapted into huge terrifying weapons in themselves, claws and pincers that can squeeze a Human body into pulp with hardly any effort. And yet those same claws can clasp gently, and can grip most weapons, from a tiny throwing dart, to the immense swords used in most primitive societies, the broadsword, the battle-axe, the scimitar. *Right: Although now* extinct, the Ptermaridi still holds a deep, subconscious terror for the Uan-irec. In their early days struggling to evolve upon Madrigallax, these giant flying reptiles were the main cause of uan-irec death and destruction. They would descend in waves upon a castle and quite literally tear the structure to pieces, killing and consuming vast numbers of the inhabitants. They were finally destroyed when the Uan-irec developed fire weapons. *Far right: Music World.* Wyath is a world of music, each natural cave, cavern, tunnel and gulley being shaped into a wind instrument so that the whole world resounds with a continual song. Scattered about the world are huge, artificial organs, such as that shown here, which are designed to allow the Uan-irec to introduce their own sounds into the symphony of nature.

spirits. To regulate the music, and to maintain the pipes and blow holes of the huge planetary organ, an entire race has been coerced and enslaved to the task of crawling throughout the system and keeping the music flowing. The race is humanoid, and of diminutive stature. Called the Mymurth, they had been at an early Stone Age level of development when the ships of the Uan-irec arrived, settled and robbed their world of one million of its members. The Mymurth that remained have been left in peace, watched over by the Uan-irec, as if in part payment for the appalling act of kidnapping. Yet any tourist granted a visa to spend time on Wyath, listening to the strange and wonderful music, should not think twice: it is remarkably easy to ignore the shambling, ragged musicians as they go about their task, ignored by the armoured forms of the warrior elite as they wander the open spaces, subdued and entranced by the melodies of the rocks.

INDEX

SYSTEM: Alphabetic word-by-word
SECTOR KEY: OR/HM/HR/N/UI
RATING: **123**/important; 456/normal;
789/pictures, captions

ACKNOWLEDGMENTS

The publishers wish to thank the
following individuals and
organizations for their kind
permission to reproduce the pictures
in this book:

Artist Partners (John Blanche) 74–75;
Sarah Brown Agency (Peter Elson) 30–
31, 43, (Nick Fox) 92 above right; Mick
Brownfield 1; Ian Flemming (Adrian
Chesterman, Penguin Books) 2–3, 20–
21, 56–57, 58–59, 68–69, 72–73, 88–89
above and below, 90–91; Folio
(Melvyn) 84, 94 above and below;
David Hardy 'ALIEN LIFEFORMS'
FROM 'THE NEW CHALLENGE OF
THE STARS', (Mitchell Beazley, 1977)
6–7 below; Jerry Leff 82; Chris Moore
54 below, 55; Harrison Rose, Dream
Masters Agency (Morris Scott Dollens)
37; Sheila Rose 'MARS' (© 1977) 12–13,
'VULCAN' (© 1979) 46–47, 'SUNRISE
ON MERCURY' (© 1977) 78–79; Thomas
Schlück (© Oliviero Berni) 'UNTITLED'
54 above left, (© Edward Blair Wilkins)
'UNTITLED' 25, 'UNTITLED' 60,
'UNTITLED' 71, (© David Hardy)
'ALIEN CONTACT' FROM THE
MAGAZINE 'FANTASY AND SCIENCE
FICTION' (June 1978) 24 below,
'UNTITLED' 28, 'CRASH LANDING'
FROM 'THE NEW CHALLENGE OF
THE STARS' (Mitchell Beazley, 1977)
83, (© Eddie Jones) 'STARSHIP
HEART OF GOLD' 4–5, 'COLONY
BETA' 64–65, 'ORION 66' 86, (© George
Jones) 'UNTITLED' 54 above right,
(© F. Jürgen Rogner) 'UNTITLED' 24
above, (© Eric Ladd) 'DRAGON LORD'
44–45, (© Carl Lundgren) 'WHITE
HART' 67, (© Morris Scott Dollens)
'AURORA ON MERCURY' 26–27, (©
Michael Whelan) 'THE MAN WHO
COUNTS' 10–11, 'BROTHER ASSASSIN'
16, 'THE FUZZY PAPERS' 41, 'WITH
FRIENDS LIKE THESE' 42, 'SHILIAN'
66, (© Graham Wildridge) 'UNTITLED'
18 above left, 'FIRST MEN ON MIMAS'
18–19 below, 'UNTITLED' 80; John
Schoenherr 7 above and below, 70
above left; Paul Stinson 36; Boris
Vallejo 'SPACE GUARDIAN' 15, 'LOCH
NESS MONSTER' 35; Young Artists (Jim
Burns) 52–53, 64, (Alan Daniels) 28–29,
(Les Edwards) 34–35, 38–39, (Peter
Goodfellow) 50, 77 below, (Colin Hay)
44, 76 below, 84–85, 95 (Peter Knifton)
18–19 above, 40–41, (Mike Masters)
92–93, (Angus McKie) 48, 74 above
and below, (Terry Oakes) 10, 14–15,
17, 30, 32, 48–49, 50–51, 60–61, 76–77
above, 80–81, 92 above left, (Tony
Roberts) 22–23, 33, 53, 62–63, 70 above
right, (Roy Virgo) 87.

The map on pages 8–9 was visualized
by Everol McKenzie and illustrated by
Jeff Alger with reproductions from
Computer Graphics (Dover
Publications) by Melvin L. Prueitt.
Index compiled by Frederick Smyth.
Our thanks are due to Vivianne Croot,
Rick Fawcett, Julia Blackburn and Reb
Linos.